COLD AS ICE

PIPER RAYNE

Cover design: RBA Designs

Line Editor: Love N Books

Proof Reader: Shawna Gavas, Behind The Writer

Cold as Ice

It may be Winter Games, but the bedroom games are about to begin...

Competing in South Korea on the world stage is hard enough.

Having to spend the entire press tour beforehand with a woman who hates me? Karma really is a bitch.

While she's spent the last four years loathing me, I've spent them ignoring the guilt that gnaws at my stomach.

All Mia Salter cares about is that I'm her brother's ex-best friend and it's her duty to hate me. The funny thing is, I barely noticed her back when she was trying to keep up with us on the slopes. Now, as both of us prepare to go for gold, I'm seeing her in a whole different light—and it involves a whole lotta different positions.

No one said the path to the Olympics would be easy.

COLD AS Ice

DEDICATION

To Ellie and Shawna.
Thank you for being faster than the Bedroom Games gang
snowboarding down a mountain.

Note to Readers: *We used Winter Classics instead of the*
trademarked names Winter Games and/or Olympics. We
did take a few creative liberties as well.

CHAPTER ONE

The crisp air whirls around the illuminated halfpipe that's glowing like a beacon out of the surrounding darkness. My board slides down to the starting position and I drop in the halfpipe. Music pounds in my ears and the snow crunches under the weight of my body. All the nerves and anxiety coursing through my veins disappear and my body shifts to autopilot. Blasting off the edge, I gain more height than my earlier practices. Cameras flash and the crowd's roars softly mingle with Eminem's "'Till I Collapse." Hitting my landing, I slide up the other side, flipping and circling in the air until my board hits the landing and then I do it again.

The camera flashes and cheers from the crowd grow distant, as does the music in my ears until I achieve the state I'm always grasping for—the centered feeling of being in the moment and completely focused on my goal. Eventually, I hit the end of the halfpipe, and fist pump in the air as I carve out my stop. Sending a small thank you upstairs for not slamming, I lift my goggles and high five a few fans lingering around the oval edge.

Unclipping my boots from my board, I stand in the designated spot, my gaze locked on the screen posting the scores. Was my run hard enough to gain me that qualifier to the Winter Classics? The hill packed with spectators grows quiet and the more the seconds tick by, the more I second guess whether my run was as good as it felt. Finally, my score lights up on the screen and the crowd roars louder than my heart did at the top of the slope.

My buddies and fellow snowboarders, Dax and Beckett, run out from the sidelines, wrestling me with their congratulations until I fall back into the snow.

"You did it!" Dax shakes me and then grabs my jacket and pulls me back up to my feet.

With his arm around my neck and big grins on our faces, we leave the area, so the next rider can make his run, but we're stopped by a reporter as soon as we clear the inflatable gates. A microphone is jammed in my face, and Dax and Beckett laugh.

"You're officially on the roster to head to Korea, Grady, how does it feel?" Nik, the boarder turned reporter since the last Winter Classics almost four years ago, smiles.

I smile in return and Dax punches my arm before him and Beckett head off. Hopefully they're standing where I am tomorrow. "It feels good," I say. "Luck was on my side."

It's the same questions every time for the past six years.

"I'm not sure many would call it luck. You rode flawlessly and you seem to top your tricks every run."

"As you know, Nik, a lot of practice in the offseason."

He pats my back. "Well, all those long hours paid off. Go rest up."

"I'll be sticking around for the night."

"No doubt to see how Matt Peterson does?" he asks with a raised brow.

Over the past year, reporters have loved to put the pressure on me over this new up-and-comer who just got off his mom's tit. He doesn't have the sponsors I do. A halfpipe wasn't carved out for him to practice on exclusively for the last year. Maybe next year will be his after I'm retired and out of the scene, but as long as I'm in it, he won't see center stage. Mark my words.

"Always have to check out my competitors." I give a laugh I hope sounds somewhat genuine. "Can't fall behind."

Nik laughs and shakes his head. "Don't forget the women are coming up in an hour. Curious about Mia Salter, she's being referred to as the woman version of you."

My stomach churns. "She's a hard trainer, I would expect nothing else."

"Many say she's here to defend her family name."

My jaw clenches and my eyes bore into Nik's. What the hell is he trying to do?

"Every boarder has their own motivations, I suppose. Nice talking to you, Nik. See you around."

I walk away, Dax and Beckett now scowling in Nik's direction. He was one of us. He was around when it all went down.

"There you have it ladies, the famous Grady Kale is the first to grab a spot on the Winter Classics team on the first qualifying event—the halfpipe. No one would argue that they didn't believe that was going to happen tonight. Now back to you, Barb."

The camera falls off the shoulder of the man filming and Nik's boots are crunching the snow seconds before he appears at my side. "Hey Rogue," he says, using my nickname. "You gotta know I have to make a spot for myself," he says.

I inhale a deep breath, and nod.

"I mean after the last Winter Classics, and Mia being Brandon's sister..."

I nod.

"Fucking sell out," Dax adds and Nik's attention turns to him.

"Stay out of it, Soups." Nik's gaze returns to mine. "I didn't mean to pick at any old wounds. The station wanted me to ask. You know it'll be a big story this year with you and Mia on the same team."

"Don't sweat it. It's no big deal." I clap him on the shoulder and feign a smile.

He nods and joins his cameraman to set up their next shot while I head to the sidelines with my friends, and prepare to watch Matt Peterson try to steal my spot.

The crowd screams their encouragement and kids hold carved out pictures of Matt as he makes his way down to the starting point.

"He's got nothing on you," Beckett says from where he stands next to me.

The fact that Dax and Beckett seem to always feel the need reassure me annoys the shit out of me. It implies that I need reassuring. The kid has guts and in this business, that's the difference between earning weight around your neck or not. But he's not seasoned. He's not ready yet.

Matt drops in the halfpipe and I don't see him as a whole—a snowboarder soaring down the wall, I see every small movement of his body. How he leans, where he tucks, his shoulder placement, how he shifts his weight, the grip on his board, his landings. The kid is choppy, and I'm not saying that because he's been in my rearview mirror all season. He flies up the south wall and all the hands in the crowd are raised from the amount of air he grabs.

"Shit, what's the kid thinking?" Dax asks next to me. All

three of us are poised to see if he'll ever stop spinning so he can actually land.

"Fuck!" Beckett says.

I wince, unable to watch as his limp body falls down to the center of the pipe. He lays down for what seems like a lifetime, but thankfully, he sits up after a few seconds. He grabs his helmet off his head and throws it. It spins like a top all the way down to the end of the pipe as trainers and medical staff run out to him. He shrugs off any assistance, unhooking himself from his board, he doesn't look to the crowd. Instead, his head is low and although I can't hear him, I guarantee the movement of his lips are him swearing at himself.

"The kid needs to try those tricks with a foam pit." Beckett shakes his head.

"But if he lands it..." Dex raises his eyebrows in my direction.

I'll need to be using my own air pillow to master that trick and stay one ahead of him.

The scores come up and he doesn't even look. Sucks, but that's what separates him from me. Keep the crazy shit for practice and never do a trick unless you've mastered it and know for certain you can land it.

"I need a drink." I grab my board and head through the crowd.

Fans and friends all stop to congratulate me. Dex and Beckett find their way to each of my sides.

"You're buying." Dex's hand lands on my shoulder.

"Aren't I always?" I deadpan.

I don't mind this time because with his competition tomorrow night, I know I'll be let off easy.

The announcer's voice crackles through the speakers,

"Next up. Women's snowboarding halfpipe. My money is on Mia Salter."

"I think the whole place would agree with you on that one," the second announcer agrees.

A picture of her flashes on the electronic board in front of me. I take a quick glance and then focus on the bar up ahead.

The queasy feeling in my stomach that sets in whenever I see or hear the Salter name makes its usual appearance. It's familiar by now, more than four years later.

Where's that damn drink?

CHAPTER TWO

I crack my neck, staring up at the snow hill littered with too many damn novice snow lovers vying for space. Preparing for the Classics jumbles my mind as all the different sides of myself push to the forefront. The responsible one that knows I'm here to do a job. The technical one that's looking at all the dips and curves of the slope and calculating the best route down. And the kid inside who's eager for a chance to mess around in the powder.

The grueling hours of training will continue after this pit stop, but I need to recharge and remember why I love this sport. There's nothing better than alone time on the slopes for that, except maybe veering off to backcountry to discover a new favorite spot.

"There you are!" Candice, my sports agent screams. Her blonde hair flies in front of her eyes from a burst of cold wind and one foot flies up in the air, her fall to the ground not far behind.

I reach out and grab her arm, unable to keep her from hitting the ground completely, but at least her head didn't meet ice.

"This is all a sign that I should only have summer athletes as my clients." She laughs at herself, standing up and brushing the snow off her ass.

Candice is bundled up like we're spending the day in Canada. Wait until she has to follow me there for events. I see a soft leather chair in the lodge in her future.

"So, where're the cameras?" I ask.

"We're heading to the back side of the mountain. They've closed off a run for two hours. Make sure you don't fall and get it right the first time."

She swings her arm through mine. Probably for her safety. At least that's what I'm telling myself because when my Hollywood agent cousin, Jagger, recommended Candice be my agent, he immediately followed up with the advice on not to mix business with pleasure.

We're making small talk when a snowmobile pulls up beside us. The guy introduces himself, grabs my board, strapping it to the machine, then holds the keys out to me.

Today must be my lucky day.

I hop on and just as I'm about to rev up the engine and hightail it where I need to go, Candice tiptoes over on her boots, careful not to slip. She slips on behind me, her thighs pressed to mine, her arms tight around my middle while her cheek is pressed against my back. "Be gentle with me," she says above the noise of the engine.

It doesn't take long before we're on the other side of the mountain. Cameras are lined up and down the hill, sure to cover every angle of my descent and the sponsor's logo has been freshly painted into the snow.

I cut the engine and Candice is off and walking with a little more confidence now since the ground isn't slick from all the traffic of a busy ski day. She talks with Hal, the Creative Director of Gasoline Energy Drinks, for a moment and then the two of them make their way over to me while I wait for my instructions.

"Grady." Hal sticks out his hand between us. "Congratulations on making the team."

"Thanks, man." I take his offering and shake. "Great to be here."

He nods. We have a good working relationship. I do what he says and try to make his life easy. He, in turn, reports back that I'm easy to work with and that the company should continue to sponsor me.

"I was just telling Candice the other skier is already up there. The two of you will board down the hill at an equal pace, skid to a stop at the bottom. Take off your goggles and say, "We're going to be on fire in Korea thanks to Gasoline Energy Drinks.""

I nod, committing my line to memory. "No back trails today?"

He laughs. "Nope. After you win gold, we'll do one." He winks, knowing I can't take the chance of injuring myself this close to the Classics, but damn if last year's promo in backcountry where we helicoptered in isn't fresh on my mind.

"Okay," Hal says when a guy about my age comes over, hops on the snowmobile and revs it. "Ollie will take you up to your starting point. Try to stay even with the other skier."

I sit down on the snowmobile, position my goggles over my eyes. "Who's the other boarder?" I ask over the engine.

Candice looks at Hal and Hal to her.

Fuck me.

"Never mind." I turn to Ollie. "Go."

He speeds up the hill, a knot stacking on top of a knot for every inch we grow closer to the top. Because I know who's going to be up there and I know there will be only hatred written all over her face. There always is.

We haven't said more than hi in the years since the... incident...and that's only when other people are present. She loathes me and I don't blame her, but it's been four years. Time for her to act like an adult and the professional athlete she wants to be.

Mia's strapping herself to her board when we pull up, her ass up in the air, front and center and hard not to appreciate. Damn, she's grown. There's no trace of the lanky body that was once under the curves she boasts now.

She straightens at the sound of the snowmobile approaching, turning to look over her shoulder with eyes so cold that it wouldn't surprise me to feel a gust of bone-chilling wind from her direction.

"Congrats on making the team," I say stiffly, stepping off the snowmobile and then bending down to strap my feet to my board.

"You as well."

Our words are stilted and formal, as if we're a pair of Englishmen preparing for a game of croquet.

"Let's shred this then." I place my goggles over my eyes, eager to get this show on the road. Nothing good can come from Mia and I having to be in each other's presence alone for any length of time. I turn toward the hill and wait for someone to give me the signal that we're ready to roll.

She says nothing else, but when I steal a glance her way, her posture speaks more than if she outright yelled at me. Her back is ramrod straight, her hands clenched into fists.

"Mia," Ollie approaches her, tapping her on the shoulder. "I need you two to face one another."

Well, hello sweetheart. I can't help but wonder what she looks like under all those layers.

Ollie gives us each a thumbs-up. "I'm going to count to three. Try to stay on pace, okay? They want you stopping at the same time."

We both nod.

His fingers go up in the air. One. Two. Three.

I leave the platform first, but she catches up to me right away. Our pace is consistent, weaving back and forth down the hill. Nothing crazy, no tricks. Just a leisurely lap down the mountain as if we have all the time in the world. I'm not sure I've done this since I was five.

Mia's the first one to hop over a mound and grab some air. I follow suit because this is boring as fuck and the hell if she'll show off and I won't. I fly up another mound and turn in the air.

I catch sight of Mia studying me under her goggles and I can only imagine she's pissed. Her competitive nature has only grown stronger over the years and I may not be close to her family anymore, but she never could take it when her brother and I left her in our dust down the mountain. She winds through the trees to her right, her body ducking and rising through the obstacles the woods present. Gutsy for a girl who just claimed her spot in the Winter Classics.

I should stay on course. Do a couple lame maneuvers I mastered at the age of ten, but... fuck that. My board follows her path and soon I weave by another tree and gain traction on her. We both fly off a shelf and flip, her air probably as high as mine. Even when Mia Salter is being crazy, she keeps it somewhat safe and cautious.

We land and continue to try to one-up each other as we fly past tree trunks that could ruin our careers, if not our lives.

I ride up one spot and the edge of my board hits a tree.

Snow spraying all over me, leaving the tree as the only spot of green on the hill.

Somewhere along the ride, we end up back on the run, me a few seconds before her. I reach the end first and carve out a spot for us at the bottom, where we take off our goggles and stare into the camera.

"We're going to be on fire in Korea thanks to Gasoline Energy Drinks," we say in unison.

"Cut." Hal stomps over, his big boots leaving indents in the snow. "What the hell was that? Turn around."

Mia and I truly make eye contact for the first time. Her eyes are a crisp sparkling blue, her lips a light pink that matches the rosiness of her cheeks and she's breathing heavily. When did she become so hot? The way she's panting from exertion makes me wonder if it's reminiscent of what she's like after she comes.

As soon as that thought enters my brain, I scrunch my forehead and give my head a shake.

Where the hell did that come from?

Mia scowls at me and a chill runs through my body. "What?" she asks, clearly annoyed.

"Hey, you two." I drop her gaze and look over at Hal. "Those are the cameras." He points up the run to where the cameras have been strategically placed along the edge of the run. "This was supposed to be the two of you out for a leisurely ride after winning your spots on the team—within camera range. Not some pissing contest over who can outdo the other through the trees."

Hal's pissed and I can't say I blame him. We wasted a good amount of time and money with our stunt.

"Now, Ollie is going to take you back up that mountain and you're going to ride down with each other, smiling and having fun. Got it?"

I nod, but it seems Mia's a harder sell.

"I can't act. That's why I snowboard," Mia says, her voice holding onto some of her earlier annoyance.

"Well, if you'd like Gasoline to continue cutting that check, channel your junior high theater class and get your ass up that hill." Hal's no shit attitude rings loud and clear.

Gasoline's been my sponsor since I was twelve. I've got my fingers crossed that they're going to build me my very own halfpipe for practicing. Damn if I'm going to fuck that up.

I head to the snowmobile, but I end up face-to-face with Mia. Holding out my hand, I smile. "Ladies first."

Her eyes might be hidden under her goggles again, but her tight lips let me see how easy it is to get under her skin.

She hops on the back, holding her board to her chest and lets Ollie take her back up the hill.

"Can we all act civilized?" Candice comes to stand at my side.

"Sure thing." I wink.

"That smirk tells me no, but listen, get this promo right and then you'll be done with one another for awhile."

"Did you know she was going to be here?" I ask, curious why she wouldn't have warned me.

She nods, grabbing her ChapStick out of her pocket and applying a layer to her lips. "Of course." She puckers her lips and then stashes the tube back in her coat pocket. "Mia is my client."

The cold air seeps into my slack-jawed mouth. "What? This is something that should've been discussed when I hired you."

"No." She shakes her head and the rumble of the snowmobile engine grows closer as Ollie makes his way back down the mountain. "She has nothing to do with you. You can both be my clients."

"You know our past." I push back all the thoughts trying to invade my brain—the regret, the shame and disappointment.

She nods. "I do."

"You're just trying to grab two big paychecks because we're the best."

A sly smile crosses her lips and she peeks up at me. "Are you admitting that Mia Salter is the best?"

I stare at her blankly unable to find words for her. No wonder Jagger suggested her, she's sharp.

Her small mittened hand pats my back. "Now, hop on that snowmobile, and do this right so you can earn both of us a paycheck."

My mind swirls like snow tumbling down in an avalanche—Candice represents both of us? It shouldn't be a problem since men and women's ad budgets don't usually mix together...if anything, sponsors pick one of each and target to each sex.

I hop on the snowmobile and without delay, Ollie flies up the hill, engine roaring.

Once it slows at the top, I jump off, securing myself to my board without much thought. It's second nature by now.

Mia's waiting for me at the top of the hill, her gaze assessing.

What's this? There's no disgusted look on her face. I doubt all those little girl flutters from the past have had a resurgence in her stomach. Not after what happened with her brother.

"I thought you hated me?" I ask, unable to resist taunting her.

Her eyes snap up to meet my gaze, her lips straightening.

"I do." She positions her pink goggles over her eyes.

I lower my own. "It looks like you were objectifying me." I slide my board back and forth over the top of the snow, anxious to get going.

"I can appreciate the view. It's no different than you did earlier when you were checking out my ass." Her tongue slides out of her mouth, licking her lips.

I've never so badly wondered what lips taste like.

Whoa. What the hell am I thinking?

I'm going to chalk that one up to the fact that I've been so busy training that getting laid has been on the back burner and right about now any female would look appetizing.

"You're seeing things. I don't check out my best friend's sister."

She glances over to Ollie who's on the radio talking to someone at the bottom of the hill.

A hollow laugh leaves her mouth into the still cold air. "You're not his best friend anymore."

Her words cut deep, but I can't let her see how deep.

We lock gazes and teeter back and forth on our boards, itching to go.

"Let me rephrase it then...I don't date my ex-best friend's sister."

"And I don't date immature assholes who only give a shit about themselves." Her lips turn up into a fake smirk.

She breaks our connection, looking down to fix her glove—not that there seemed to be anything wrong with it to begin with. "Ollie!" she yells.

He holds his hand up in the air, indicating that it'll be another minute.

"Getting to be a bit of a diva, are you? I mean you don't even have a medal yet."

Her smirk vanishes and even I know that was hitting below the belt. But damn if Mia and all that she represents doesn't bring out the worst side of me.

"That's all going to change. Care to wager a little bet about who will pick up more gold at the Winter Classics?"

I laugh, shaking my head. I could easily win that bet.

"Are we talking sexual favors when I win?" I don't know why I can't stop myself from baiting her.

She glances behind me for a second and then grabs a hold of her earbud, readying to put it in her ear. I assume Ollie's on his way over.

"I wouldn't sleep with you even if you had a nine-inch dick," she spits out.

I grin. "You've heard the rumors I take it? I'm disappointed to know they're shortchanging me. Ten inches and girth doesn't disappoint." I wink.

"UGH!" she screams.

I laugh.

This girl has always been too easy to rile up.

Ollie approaches, looking over to me from the corner of his eyes.

"You okay, Mia?" he asks.

"Let's just do this." Again, she rocks her board side-to-side.

"They're ready for you guys," he says. We watch as he counts us down again.

Mia and I might not agree on anything, but we each move down the hill at a consistent pace suggesting that we might agree on one thing—we both want this to be over, so we can go back to pretending the other doesn't exist.

CHAPTER THREE

"Who is that?" I ask Dax as he comes out of the lodge. My stomach growls at the mouthwatering cheeseburger he's just about finished devouring.

Stuffing the last piece in his mouth, he positions his goggles on top of his head and squints in the direction I was looking. "Not sure. They all look the same, but even with those snow pants on, I can tell that her ass is definitely slapable."

Dax has great vision, but you could be halfway from here to Denver and still notice this girl. Then she does her signature move. One she perfected especially for the Winter Classics. One that the announcers won't stop raving about.

And suddenly I'm glad I didn't get in on that cheeseburger when my stomach pitches. Because again, I caught myself checking out my ex-friend's little sister.

"Come on. Let's go get a beer." I knock Dax's shoulder, but he doesn't budge.

Dax swallows his last mouthful of burger. "You're going to have to face her eventually. Now that the Winter Classics are coming up we're going to be around the women's team more often," he says, zipping his coat. "If I were you, I'd be searching for the quickest way to get her out of those snow pants."

I roll my eyes. *As if.* "I don't need her shitty attitude today."

I unhook the straps of my board, step out and start walking toward the lodge.

"You're never a pussy, what's the deal?" Dax follows behind.

"Nothing, I've seen her, okay? It's not like I've gotten through these past few years without seeing her. I just prefer not to." Why am I even explaining myself? Dax should get it.

He shrugs. "If I leave this slope, coach will be slapping my ass...and not in a good way."

I forgot that Dax got in trouble for having more fun than training last week and that his qualifier event got delayed until tomorrow.

"Shit. Go."

"I'll meet you in the bar in twenty minutes."

I raise my eyebrows. "Twenty minutes and coach will still have your ass. I'll catch up to you tonight."

My gaze veers to the halfpipe, seeing Mia at the bottom, smiling and laughing with some girl I don't know.

"We could double date."

I snap my eyes back to Dax. "Go!"

He holds his hands up in the air, heading to the far chairlift.

"There you are," the high-pitched voice of my agent slaps me on the back. Not that I'm complaining about the new sponsor I acquired last week because of her.

"Hey, Candice, I was just heading out."

She's bundled up in her snow gear. Boots, tight ass jeans and a long coat. A USA hat and glove set she obviously just bought, not vibing with the rest of her designer outfit.

"No, you're not. We have a late lunch meeting this afternoon."

I rack my brain for a second. I would remember a meeting since I had plans of being on the slopes all day. "I don't have anything on the schedule."

"It's an impromptu one. I worked some magic and I think you'll be happy to hear what I got for my two top clients." She pulls out her tube of ChapStick, unable to take the cap off with her gloved hands, but she keeps trying anyway.

I take the ChapStick from her and pop the cap off. "Thanks." She coats her lips again. "I've never been this dry in my entire life."

"Two top clients?" I ask, dreading her answer.

"Yeah, you and Mia Salter. Now come on, she's meeting us at the restaurant."

Candice pulls on my arm, but my feet stay planted to the ground. She's got to be kidding me. Mia and me sharing a table? We'll be lucky to make it past drinks. Does she think because we cordially made it down the hill yesterday that means we're cool with one another?

"How long has Mia been your client?" My boots click on the concrete pathway to the lodge.

"Well," she says, waiting for me to catch up. "Mia was my first sports client."

I think for a moment, if Candice got Mia to hold all those companies on her board and the sponsorship with one of the biggest brands, I guess my cousin Jagger picked the right person to represent me. I shouldn't make waves and fuck it up.

"I have to change, I'll meet you there in fifteen."

She nods, pulling out her ChapStick *again* as she stares over at the slopes. "Sounds good. I'll order you a water."

"If Mia Salter is at the table, you can order me a vodka tonic and leave the bottle at the table."

She purses her lips and shakes her head. "You two need to learn to get along."

I ignore her, heading into the lodge.

It'll be a cold day in hell before Mia forgives me for what I've done.

I WALK into Warm 'N Toasty, the comfy log cabin restaurant with a large double-sided fireplace nestled in the middle and comfy leather booths lining the outside edges of the room. It's the go-to for most of the riders because of its proximity to the chairlifts and loose dress code.

Though, Dax might've forced the owner's hand when he showed up last year in only his boxer briefs. To his defense, it was an unseasonably warm winter day. The girls weren't complaining.

My eyes scan the room until I spot Candice's arm up in the air, waving me over, while a sour looking Mia sits across from her. I weave through the tables, fist-pumping and high-fiving a few fellow boarder's hands. They all study where I'm going with curiosity when I don't stop to chat.

Mia has one yoga pant clad leg propped up on the edge of the bench and a slice of pickle an inch from being devoured into her mouth.

"Ladies," I say, shrugging off my coat and hanging it on the hooks between the booths.

I slide in on the other side of the booth next to Candice. Mia doesn't even so much as glance in my direction.

"I got you a water." Candice eyes the tall bottle of water on the table in front of me.

"Thanks." I snap the seal open, downing a hefty gulp, my gaze trained on Mia the entire time.

She bites off a piece of the pickle, showing her teeth like she's a guard dog who's cornered me. When she's done chewing, she brings her drink to her lips and sips it.

I turn my attention back to Candice. "So, are we celebrating something?" I ask.

"Great idea." Candice raises her hand to flag down the waitress.

The red-haired waitress, Natalie, stops at the edge of our table, an array of empty hot chocolate mugs on her tray. "Hey Rogue," she says and then looks across the booth from me. "Mia." Her eyes widen and she does a double take at the both of us.

Yeah, you got it right. Grady Kale and Mia Salter are sitting at the same table together.

"What can I get you?" she grants Candice her undivided attention.

"I need a bottle of champagne."

"I don't drink champagne," I mumble.

"Me either," Mia murmurs.

Candice's attention moves from me to Mia and then back to Natalie. "Well, I do. Just a glass then."

"I'll grab that for you now." Her hand lands on the edge of the table, pausing for a second. "Rogue, do you want anything else?"

Mia scoffs, but when my gaze shoots in her direction, she pretends to concentrate on her Bloody Mary.

"Um...yeah, Nat, can you grab me an Amstel?"

Nat's knuckles knock the wood table. "Sure thing."

She's a good distance away before Mia's gaze stops following her. She has to know Nat, she's the owner's daughter and one of Mia's biggest fans.

"Surprise, surprise, another female who caters to Grady."

Candice ignores Mia's snide comment. "What's up with the Rogue thing?" she asks, sipping her mix drink.

Mia snickers, twirling her celery around in her drink. "That's what they call him because he only cares about himself." She looks across the table, daring me to argue with her.

"How's that?" Candice asks, a little warily.

I bet she knows for sure now that having both of us as clients is a bad idea.

"My friends started calling me that when I was younger because of the tricks I'd do. I'd try stuff no one else would dare to." My eyes bore over at Mia, but apparently her drink is still more interesting than me because she can't meet my gaze. "I set myself apart."

"More like you isolated yourself. I think your nickname should be changed to Ogre." She laughs to herself, pulling the piece of celery from her drink, smiling to herself.

"Okay, you two. I know there's history, but we have to remain professional," Candice says.

"Ogre, huh? I don't think you were staring at me yesterday like I was Shrek."

Nat comes back, placing a glass of champagne in front of Candice and a beer down in front of me. I lift the bottle to my lips as Nat slides a plate of pickles, celery, olives and a pepperoni stick in front of Mia.

"Thanks, Nat." She grabs the pepperoni stick and

chomps down on it aggressively. "I love biting down on a good piece of meat."

Nat glances to me and then hurries off to help some other customers. I wish I could go with her.

"There wouldn't be a problem if you kept us in our assigned corners," I say to Candice.

"Unfortunately, that's not a possibility. Why do you think I'm celebrating?" She lifts her champagne.

Mia's foot falls to the floor and she lets the celery plop back down into her glass then leans forward, fixing her eyes on Candice.

I swivel in my seat, giving Candice all my attention.

"What exactly are you celebrating?" I ask.

Candice's smoky grey eyes move between the two of us and then she plasters on the fakest smile I've ever witnessed, and I've seen many. "You were both chosen to represent the snowboarding team on a press tour. Yay!"

Mia leans back in the booth, downing the rest of her Bloody Mary. "Not going to happen."

Once again, Mia Salter and I see eye-to-eye about something.

CHAPTER FOUR

"Hear me out." Candice sits up straighter, squaring her shoulders.

"We have to train," Mia says, and though I won't voice it, she's right.

"Are we going to cause you to become an alcoholic?" I ask, the corner of my lips quirking up.

"Can you be serious for once?" Mia spits out.

I tilt my head. "Relax. They can't make us do anything we don't want to do."

Mia disregards me and challenges Candice, who is back to sipping her champagne.

"No, I'm just going to need a little buzz to deal with the two of you." Candice waves her hand between us. "Now, be quiet and let me get this out." Her hand falls back to the table and neither one of us says anything. "You are the best in the women." She looks from Mia to me. "And you're the best in men." Her gaze volleys between the two of us. "You'll still have time to train, but you were going to be doing promotions anyway, the only difference is, you'll be doing them together."

"But—" Mia tries to interject.

Candice shakes her head. "You'll model the outfits the team will wear when they're competing, you'll do the interviews. It's an honor to represent your country and your team this way. I'm sorry you guys, but did you really think that either one of you would get out of these Winter Classics without having to face one another?"

"A girl can dream," Mia quips with eyes narrowed in my direction.

"Well, I'm not a genie in a bottle, so you'll have to suck this up. Most of your appearances will be around the other qualifiers, but you'll be traveling to New York and L.A., too. Together. In every interview, the two of you will be seated side by side. So, might as well practice your smiles and non-verbal body language now. We have a photo shoot planned in a week when we head to Utah."

She leans back in her seat, lets a big sigh escape and reaches for her champagne.

I want to argue, but she's right. It is an honor and once upon a time I didn't think anything like this would be possible for myself, so I'll have to make the best of it.

"Send me the itinerary, I'll get it handled, but every moment I'm not with the press, I'll be training."

Mia slides out of the booth. "Me, too." She walks away without so much as a goodbye. Like I'd expect any less. She acts like she's the fucking queen and she's yet to prove herself in a Winter Classics.

"Thanks, Candice. You ready for weeks of exploring your parental disciplining skills?"

She downs the remainder of her glass of champagne. "I told them it was a bad idea, but" —she looks back to the doors and my way— "there's more that I didn't tell Mia."

The beer sits heavy in my stomach. The only thing worse would be to add Mia's brother, Brandon to this mix.

"They like the angle of you two being a love match. You know...a couple."

I laugh sardonically. "There's no love match."

A soft smile creases her lips. "They'll be prying in the interviews. The two of you are unattached attractive young people with a history—"

"Of hating each other."

Her hand grabs mine and in the last few months I've known Candice, I've never seen her so intense. "I don't think you hate her."

Maybe not, but self-preservation insists I do.

"She needs to grow up. Is there anything else?"

Her smile widens. "There is. I have good news."

"Finally. You were starting to be my biggest buzz kill."

She laughs and her hand leaves mine, the moment of seriousness fading.

"Norton is building you a halfpipe to train."

I smile. I hoped they would, but it takes being on top to make it happen. I may talk a good game and the standings might say I'm on top, but I can't help but wonder sometimes.

"It will be ready when we get to Utah. Just an FYI though, they only built one." Her perfectly done eyebrows arch up to her hairline.

"Sucks for Mia I guess." I slide out of the booth. "I better go practice while I have the time."

"It'd be a nice gesture if you allowed her to practice on it, too."

I place my hands on the edge of the table and narrow my eyes at Candice. "Would she do the same for me?"

Her shoulders sag. We both know the answer.

"Have a good afternoon, Candice. It's a great day to be out on the slopes."

She laughs. "I'm good with the bar. I'll leave the powder to you and Mia."

I should be ecstatic about having my own personal half-pipe to train on. I'll have a leg up to practice but for some damn reason the fact that Mia won't have one dampens that excitement. She's been back in my life for forty-eight hours and already her presence is stripping me of my happiness.

I HITCH a ride up the lift wishing I had more than just a beer in my stomach. Spotting my buddy Beckett waiting to use the halfpipe, I slide up to him.

"Rogue, what's up man?" A skier I don't know says as he passes.

"Great ride last night," his buddy says with his fist out and ready. I knock knuckles and they carry on their way.

"What's up, Hoff?"

Beckett glances over his shoulder and nods. "Hey, saw you in the restaurant." The cocky ass smile on his lips makes me wish I didn't seek him out.

"Yeah, turns out princess is my agent's client as well."

His mouth hangs open. "You didn't know?"

I shake my head. "Why are you at the halfpipe?"

Beckett is a slopestyle boarder, meaning he does all those fancy tricks but not in the halfpipe like I do.

"Change of pace. Trying to reenergize myself." He prepares himself as he moves up in line. "Why are you changing the subject?" His eyes hold that glint of curiosity they always do whenever the Salter name comes up.

Beckett and I became friends at the Winter Classics

four years ago. He was my roommate, so all he knows are the rumors. He's a good enough friend not to pry and bother me for details, so I have to assume he only knows whatever Dax has told him.

"Because I don't want to talk about the fact that I'll be spending the next six weeks sitting next to that subject while we promote the snowboarding team around the country."

His mouth opens wide enough for an entire snowman to fit inside. "You're shittin' me?"

"Nope." I adjust myself on my board, preparing to ride right after Beckett.

He clamps me on the shoulder. "Sorry, man. That sucks, but maybe it'll help you all heal and put the whole thing behind you."

I mentally scoff. There's no getting past the events I put into motion.

"Save your California beach bum one love bullshit for yourself." I push him lightly in the chest.

He laughs, sliding backward to his starting spot. Seconds later he's off.

Beckett's from California, and even though he doesn't have blonde hair everything else about him screams 'hey, brah, surf on.' Hence the reason we call him Hoff—like from Baywatch.

"He's nailing it," the rider behind me says.

He's right, Beckett should be competing in the halfpipe *and* the slopestyle. I place my earbud in my ear and ready myself for some fun.

Once he reaches the bottom, he waves his hands in a challenge my way.

"Get him, Rogue," the guy behind me says so loud I can hear him over my earbud.

Snow crunches under my board as I drop into the half-pipe, but this time the music isn't enough to push my past away. My mind envisions sitting next to Mia at all the interviews. Plastering a smile on our faces so people don't suspect what they should. That four years ago, the Salter and the Kale families flipped from friends to enemies faster than a tossed coin. And I'm responsible.

I'm high up in the air, turning my double cork when my mind finally decides to get with the game, but it's too late. My shoulder hits the hard ice first, but my body follows, sliding down until I lay limp in the middle of the halfpipe.

I shake my head and stand to my feet, holding my shoulder while I continue down the slope. When I reach the bottom, a medic is already approaching.

"I'm good." My hand grips my shoulder.

"Let's just do a mobility check on it," the girl says.

"She's right." Beckett unstraps himself from his board, helping me off mine and grabbing it to follow me and the medic.

A crowd of onlookers watch, half probably wanting me to be hurt and the other half scared that I might be. Only one face in the group stands out like the sun is shining above her head alone. Mia's eyes don't hold their usual anger as she watches the medics escort me to the first aid station. But there's no way they can be holding compassion. Snow must have gotten in my eyes because she loathes me.

And she has every right to.

CHAPTER FIVE

"Grady, gonna win gold?" Mr. Kettle asks, positioning the mini chalkboard listing the specials outside his door. The butcher slaps me on the back as I walk by his shop.

"I hope." I smile and continue my way down the small downtown street of my hometown.

A ski town would best describe where I grew up. Growing up everyone was either a skier or snowboarder because there isn't much to do in this town. Cedarwood, Vermont is known for small bed and breakfasts, small lodges. During the winter, the streets line with tourists who love Mr. Kettle's beef jerky, or Ms. Greer's chocolates. Kids skate in the square while their dads drink coffee under the heaters and their moms shop in the boutiques that are really just rows of overpriced homemade goods that help to keep the town alive.

I should know how much the people of Seasalt depend on the tourists. My parent's own Cozy Cocoa Cottage, a ten-bedroom bed and breakfast which paid for all my equipment and training before any sponsors came aboard.

"Grady!" Mr. Ecker screams from across the street. His arm up in a wave with his pipe in the other free hand.

"Morning, Mr. Ecker."

"I heard you and Mia are the hot tickets this year. Do our town proud." I give him a wane smile and he heads back into his tobacco shop.

Hoping to dodge anyone else, I duck into the Cup of Beans coffee shop, crossing my fingers they'll be too busy to recognize me, or at least to corner me into a conversation.

"GRADY KALE!" A voice booms from the back of the small cafe and before I can even gather my senses, two big burly arms wrap around me and lift me up off the ground.

"Hey, Olson," I say, looking at the small group of customers obviously not understanding why this, six foot six, three-hundred-pound guy is excited enough to bear hug me.

"When did you get back? How long are you here for?"

"Hey, O, mind putting me down?"

His deep laugh rumbles and my feet land on the cement floor. He ruffles my hair like I'm ten and he's the uncle I haven't seen in ages.

"Just the weekend. Injured my shoulder, so I took the time to come home."

"Shit. Did I hurt you?" He eyes both my shoulders, but I wave off his concern. It's a sprain which just needs rest—still it sucks.

"Nah. I'm good."

He smacks me on the back. "Always are. Hear you're gonna represent Seasalt Springs again in the Winter Classics." He rounds the corner of the counter, grabbing a cup and pouring me a coffee. Without asking, he opens the back of the pastry display case, reaching toward the last of their famous Spandauers with chocolate pouring from the middle.

"No way, O, I'm training."

He glances at me from behind the case, crinkles his bushy eyebrows and then grabs two with the wax paper in his hand.

"You're on a break," says the man who samples too many of his own goods.

Not that I'd say that to my Danish friend.

Handing me the plate and the coffee he nods to the back of the cafe at an empty table.

"Here." I balance the plate and the cup to pull out my wallet.

"It's on the house."

"Come on, let me pay."

He shakes his head. "Think of it as my congratulations."

My shoulders deflate. "I haven't won anything yet."

The bell rings over the café door and his gaze shifts to over my shoulder, the easy smile that's always plastered on his face falling short.

I glance over my shoulder and a long stream of air leaves my lungs. "Fuck," I murmur.

"Want me to sneak you out back?" O asks me, and without an answer, he steps in front of me, blocking me from the intruder.

"I'm sorry, you're not welcome here," he greets them in a foreign manner.

"It's fine, O." I look the unwelcome customer in the eye. I'd remember him anywhere. Mr. Weazel, the man who pointed a finger at me as an asshole who doesn't have the character a snowboarder is supposed to possess. Like the fact that I want to win is a bad thing. The man uses his keystrokes and small blog like a gun or knife to injure people.

"Olsen, I need you," a cook from the back calls out to him, but Olsen ignores him in favor of towering over the small beady-eyed man in front of us.

"I'm good," I tell Olsen and he wavers slightly before ultimately heading to the back to help out his staff.

"So, Mr. Kale, I wasn't expecting you to return until after the town holds the parade."

"Well, as I'm sure you've heard, I injured my shoulder. Might as well see the fam before I head off to Korea." I sip my coffee and walk by him deliberately leaving my shoulder inches from him. I lean in close. "You going to write some more bullshit stories to try and get some eyeballs on your little blog?"

He backs away to gain a few inches of space. Without his computer, he's like a skittish kitten.

"Tell me, you ever head over to the Salty River Lodge? It's not lost on me that you haven't been by Brandon's place since shortly after the accident." His voice holds an arrogance that's begging my fist to gut check him.

"Even if I did, I wouldn't tell you."

His eyes narrow and he locks gazes with me. He has no idea yet that Mia is my sidekick for the tour and I wish like hell I could be there when he finds out that the gossip he's profited off of the last four years is about to die.

"You and Mia at the same Winter Classics will be...classic."

"Is that gonna be your headline? Real original."

"How about *Is Mia Salty on Grady? The Tell-All Story.*"

"You don't even know the story so don't pretend you do."

A smug expression creases the corners of his lips. "Well,

Brandon Salter has granted me an exclusive. He should be here." He weaves by me to check out the clock behind the counter. "Any minute now."

My throat closes up and my body warms from something other than the coffee. Hearing my former friend's name from this weasel's lips steals my confidence.

After the accident, this creep wrote all about how irresponsible Brandon was with taking risks and how anyone could have seen it coming. I didn't find out about it until I had returned home from the previous Winter Classics months later. Maybe Brandon finally had enough and is willing to talk about who's really to blame for what happened.

I'd search for the nearest exit if this guy wasn't watching my every move like he's a vulture about to eat roadkill. I'll never grant him the satisfaction of knowing he's getting under my skin.

"Like a guardian angel, O hollers from the back. "Grady, your mom called. Can you bring back a pound of coffee and some danishes for her?"

I nod and wave my hand at Olsen. He has no idea how much he just saved my ass. "See you, Weazel. Keep publishing crap no one gives a shit about and I'll keep doing what I do. Maybe I'll wave to you when I roll by on my float in the town parade this year." I wink just to irritate him.

I head to the back, grab the box O hands off to me.

"Thanks, man."

"Saves your parents a trip." O stuffs another bag in there and hands me a fresh coffee. "Since the weasel ruined your first order."

"Thanks, O, you're the best."

He nods. "Come back though, okay. I need an updated picture with your signature for my wall."

I laugh. "Got it." I head out the back door determined to push Weazel to the back of my mind, along with everyone else. It's too painful to dwell on.

***

IT'S late and my parents, along with all the guests have gone to bed for the night, so I make myself comfortable in the quiet and dark bed and breakfast and use my phone to catch up on my emails and social media. The incident with Weazel is still rattling around my brain and before I can convince myself that what I'm about to do is a bad idea, I find myself on his blog page.

A picture of Brandon sits front and center. *An Athlete's Family Legacy* is the title of the post. Fuck Weazel and his insane notion about that night. I click off quickly before reading anything else. Brandon and I might not be friends anymore, but I know him and the last person he'd ever confess my sins to would be Weazel.

CHAPTER SIX

The following week I'm back in Utah, heading into the photo shoot, my nerves on edge. I just got clearance to go back to training which is a good thing because sampling O's wares for the past week hasn't done me any favors. I'm itching to get back on the hill and not here doing a photo shoot like a damn Ken doll.

"Hey, Grady Kale, right?" A cute, blonde approaches me, glasses resting on the edge of her nose, an iPad in her hands.

"Yeah." I switch my coffee to my other hand and hold my free hand out in front of me.

She shakes my hand and shoots me what I imagine is her best flirtatious smile. "If you want to follow me, I'll take you to wardrobe."

She swivels on her plaid Converse and heads down the hall. At least the eye candy isn't bad here. All hope is not lost.

We reach a door halfway down with a piece of paper taped to the outside that says "Snowboarders." "Here you are." She stops and turns to face me, arm extended toward the door.

"Thanks."

"So, get changed and I'll be back to take you to set. As far as I know, you're the first to arrive."

I nod. "Thanks."

She stands there, rocking back on her Converse, her eyes looking me over like I'm a lollipop in her favorite flavor. Someone should tell her it won't take too many licks to get to my center.

My hand rests on the doorknob and I smile and nod. Spending the day flirting with a piece of eye candy is one thing, but I don't need any bad press right now, nor do I have the time or headspace to deal with dating someone before the Winter Classics are over.

She scurries away, looking a little embarrassed that I caught her checking me out. I blow out a sigh and open the door to a fucking wet dream. The blonde might not do it for me, but I wouldn't mind the naked brunette in front of me getting to the center. Sad to say, it might only take her one lick.

"Get the fuck out!" Mia screams and I swing the door shut just as something hits the other side of it.

The door may be closed, but my mind won't erase what it just saw. I'll be meditating on that mental picture the next time I beat off. Definite medibation material. Get what I did there?

Mia Salter has definitely grown up. Her tits would fill my hands, and the curves of her hips beg me to hold them as she rides me. Her pale skin revealing she spent most of her summer in New Zealand training.

I wait a minute and knock.

"Come in," she says, and I've known her long enough to know it's through gritted teeth.

I cover my eyes, pretending I'm not looking and step into the room.

"I'm dressed," she spits out.

My hand falls and sure enough, she's now decked out in her designated snow gear for the Winter Classics and all those curves and perfect tits are hidden away under layers of warmth.

"I was hoping we were playing a game of I'll show you mine if you show me yours." I can't help but tease her. It comes naturally to me since it was how it always was between us growing up. I'm surprised that even after all this time, that hasn't changed.

Her face twists into a 'get a life' expression and she sits down in front of the make-up chair, brushing out her long brown hair.

"You forget, I've seen yours." She raises her eyebrows as she stares at me through the reflection in the mirror.

I cock my head. It takes a minute for me to figure out when Mia would've seen my goods. Then the whole dare to streak board down the bunny hill when we were younger floats to the surface of my brain. Damn that brother of hers.

By the time I've remembered, my gaze finds hers and her face bears a smug expression.

"I've grown—considerably since then. In all the ways that count."

To my surprise, she giggles and her hairbrush stops moving. "I do vaguely remember you mentioning something about ten inches...you know, those that talk about it are usually the ones with a four-inch pickle." Pickle pops out of her mouth with emphasis.

"Want me to grab a ruler?" Grabbing the hem of my T-shirt, I strip it off my body and my fingers go for the button on my jeans.

She rolls her eyes, but I don't miss the pink flush to her cheeks. Mia stands, rounding the makeup chair and visions of her falling to her knees to inspect my dick size surface before she opens the door and walks out.

I'm pretty sure she's not getting a ruler.

***

AFTER GETTING MYSELF DRESSED, I step out of the dressing room. I can see why Mia went the nude route under the outfit. It's hot as shit, I'm sweating to death in my boxers.

The small blonde runs down the hallway, relief washing through her non-verbal signals. "There you are. Mia said you weren't coming out until someone found a ruler or something?" Her face is scrunched up in confusion.

I bite back a grin.

"Do you need one? I've searched everywhere and all I can find is a measuring tape. Will that do?" She pulls a metal retractable measuring tape out of her pocket.

"No, that most definitely won't do."

Her lips turn down. "I'm sorry. I can go out and buy one…"

"No worries, I'm good."

Her entire body shifts from iron rod back to jelly goo. "Phew. I was so worried."

"What would've happened if I wanted a ruler and you couldn't find one?"

She stares up at me like she's trying to figure out a hard math problem. "I guess I thought you'd be mad."

"Over a ruler?"

She shrugs and stammers a bit before she finally says, "Miss Salter...she said that you can get really irate if I don't do everything exactly how you want it...I didn't want to mess up."

I chuckle. The poor thing. "Miss Salter is fucking with you. Actually, she's fucking with me. Ignore anything she says."

She lets out a stream of air and seems to relax a bit. "Oh, thank goodness."

"What do you say we get this over with?"

She nods and I step around the shy blonde I think might be having her first day on the job, and head straight to the photo shoot. Mia's already posing with her board, a smile that's never directed my way, lighting up her face.

It hits me like a fist to the center of my chest, stealing my breath, how truly beautiful she is now that she's a woman. Instead of scolding her for telling stories to the assistant, I want to spank her. Her features are soft, the camera flashes illuminate her soft brown eyes that still hold a hint of mischief to them. She's a grown-up version of her younger self. The girl I remember with braids in her hair now has cascading dark brown waves falling past her shoulders. Her teeth are as white as newly fallen snow and straight as the steep cliffs of the mountains.

I should look away. Any minute now she's going to glance over to me and see me gawking at her. But I can't pull my gaze away because a part of me wants to bottle up this moment and carry it with me, so I can pull it out and relive it whenever I want.

As I predicted, her head turns my way and I don't react fast enough. Bam, her eyes are seared to mine.

Look away.

Fucking, look away.

As much as I scream at myself in my head, my gaze won't leave hers and the weird thing is, hers isn't leaving mine. Her tongue slides out of her mouth and my dick grows an inch. A wet path coats her lips and my taste buds kick into overdrive, desperate to know what she tastes like. Is she a mint or cinnamon girl? While all these questions are swirling in my head and I'm trying to decide what I would taste if my lips could land on hers, a man pops up in front of me with a sponge with some brown shit on it.

"What the?" I dodge his approach.

Mia's laughter rings throughout the big open space and the cameras click away. That'll probably be the best picture out of the bunch.

"Makeup," the tall, platinum blond guy says to me, the sponge inching closer to my face.

"I'm good, man." I raise my hand in front of me hoping he'll back off.

"Well, you're very white. Let's try to get some rosy cheeks." His smile does nothing to ease me.

"I'm a snowboarder."

"Exactly, the sun still shines on you up on those mountains," he says, finally landing the sponge on my forehead. The gook slides around my face, his pressure a little firmer around my nose and eyes. How do women wear this shit?

"I didn't realize this photoshoot was going to turn me into a Ken doll."

He stops and steps back, placing his free hand on his hip. "Now don't be such a crank. My job is to make you gorgeous and I never fail at my job."

"Oh, I don't know, James, some would say he's already gorgeous." Mia takes a seat in the chair next to me.

"He's got that rugged male appeal, I'll give him that." James leans back, appraising me once more like he might have missed an attractive feature or two on the first look. "Half boy next door, half mountain man."

Without another word, he pulls out a brush and starts putting more shit on my face.

"I remember when that face couldn't even grow any facial hair." Mia giggles next to me, bringing the coffee cup to her lips.

"I remember when you stuffed your bra."

She chokes on the coffee, leaning forward and letting it drop to the floor.

"Man, you guys really are enemies, huh?" James asks.

Neither of us says anything for a beat.

"She's not my enemy," I murmur.

The truth is I don't know what she is these days. Growing up, I always had a fondness for Brandon's little sister. She was four years younger than us and constantly trying to keep up with our shenanigans. I looked out for her the same way her own brother did and if anyone was stupid enough to mess with her I would have fucked them up. After the accident...well, truth is I made it a point never to see them. Any of the Salters. I didn't want to make an already difficult situation more difficult. And the odd time over the past couple of years that I've run into Mia, it's been clear she hates me for what happened to her brother. Which is totally justified. Which means I have no idea why I'm just noticing now the woman that Mia has developed into.

The blonde from earlier rushes over with a wad of paper towels, cleaning up the mess.

"I'm sorry," Mia says, "but you can blame him." She thumbs toward me and the blonde's eyes cast my way for a second and then back to the floor.

"It's okay. Um... Grady, you're up soon." Eyeing Mia's cup, she directs all attention to her. "Did you want more?"

"No, thank you, Nel, too much caffeine and I'll be bouncing off the walls."

The blonde who I now know is Nel, laughs. "Well, let me know if you need anything else."

"Thanks." Mia leans back. "Oh wait, did you ever find that ruler for Grady, Nel?" she asks.

"Ruler?" James mumbles, his fresh minty breath centimeters away from me, that annoying brush still dabbing here and there on my skin.

"Jesus." I roll my eyes.

Mia glances at me beside her, a smile teasing her lips.

"No, but Mr. Kale said it was okay, he didn't need one," Nel responds in a polite and professional voice.

"Oh, okay then. Thanks, Nel." Mia turns her attention to the man currently trying to poke my eye out with a make-up brush. "Tell me, James. Is it a male thing to measure your dick?"

The small brush pokes me in the eye.

"Motherfuc—"

"Shit. Sorry. Keep your eye closed." James's thumb traps my eyelid closed. "And sweetie, no, it's not like you walk into a gay bar and the bouncers measure your dick before you get in. They come in all shapes and sizes, but what really matters is what you do with it."

"Well, this guy here thinks his is perfect."

James's eyes dip down between my legs. "I wouldn't bet against him, darling."

Mia rolls her eyes, but the pink flush of her cheeks can't be missed and I can't help but wonder—why is she still talking about my dick?

CHAPTER SEVEN

With my face feeling like it's covered in dried-out cake frosting, I grab hold of the snowboard and step into the photo shoot area. Mia joins me minutes later with a fresh coat of makeup on her face. Not like she needed it.

"Give me a minute to set up your shot." The photographer moves between the camera and the lights, talking with his assistant.

The two of us stand there with the green screen behind us, looking anywhere but at each other.

"You training later?" I ask, hoping to fill the void of awkward silence that's developed between us.

She glances at me and then the ground. "No, the halfpipe has been a killer to get on at night. Not worth it to wait forever for only one run."

That was the wrong question to ask since I've been boarding down my own halfpipe Gasoline Energy Drinks built for me the past few days. Now I'm going to seem like a dick if I don't invite her. Not that I think she'd take me up on the offer. She's stubborn, but she'd be an idiot not to at least use me for that.

"I saw your buddy the other day," she says.

"Who? Dax?"

She shakes her head, a smirk playing on her lips.

"Well, I guess I'm using the word buddy loosely." She pauses for dramatic effect. "Peterson. He's really trying to nail that trick he's calling Peterson's Bag of Nuts."

Mia's not the first to fill me in on Peterson's endeavor to complete a new trick in order to win gold. If I said I wasn't scared of standing to his right on a platform at the Winter Classics, I'd be lying.

Mark my words, he'll never be invited to my halfpipe.

"Well, I wish him luck."

I check the photographer's progress with the hopes he'll be ready to click his camera so we can get on with this and I get back to my halfpipe and out of my head.

"No, you don't." She laughs. "Come on. He's your biggest competition and he's half your age."

I sit down on the stoop that's there for us to put our leg up. "Watch it with the age. I just turned twenty-six."

She laughs again, a sweet sing-song type of laugh that sends a rush of exhilaration through my veins. "That just about makes you a dinosaur in this world. Peterson's a child, but he's got just enough guts to pull off that trick and you know it."

I shrug. Does she really expect me to admit it?

"I have guts, too."

Her eyes widen and she sits down in front of me. "Yeah you do, but he's got the whole teenage 'I'm invincible' belief that we don't have anymore."

I nod. She's got a point.

"I'm the reigning champ. I'm not worried about some

newbie that'll probably choke when his big moment arrives." The lie comes out convincingly enough.

"Ready guys," the photographer announces.

Thank God.

Mia gets up on her hands and knees, crawling my way and then slowly rises up to her feet. "You as confident in that bet as the other one?" Her eyes dip between my legs.

"I'd take that bet every day and twice on Sunday."

"Guess we'll find out who's the best in front of millions of people." She rests her arm on her board and her finger pats her lips. "How's your shoulder?"

I stand and the photographer's assistant takes Mia's board from her momentarily.

"Is that concern I detect in your tone?" Could it be that Mia doesn't hate me as much as I thought?

She laughs but this time it holds an evil edge. "No, I just want to make sure you don't drop me when I'm on your back."

She nods towards the photographer's set-up.

"So, Grady you stand in front of the stool, Mia you step up and onto Grady's back," the photographer says. "I want huge smiles, and Mia, make sure you do your signature hang ten sign."

Mia shoots me smug look and I get myself into position. She hops onto my back, her weight barely registering, but when I have her legs hooked in my arms, the smell of honey that can only be her, has my dick waking up in my pants.

The assistant hands Mia her board and she positions it in front of us.

"Why don't you head over to my halfpipe with me tomorrow?"

"Nooo..." She draws out in a breathy whisper in my ear.

"All right, if you don't want to join, cool."

Her legs tighten around my waist and the photographer's assistant rushes toward us with some contraption he's using to measure the light or something. I mean I can hold Mia until the cows come home, but neither of these two seem like they're in any particular hurry to get this over with.

"I didn't say that," she snaps.

"If you're waiting for me to beg you, it's not going to happen." I adjust her body and get her higher up my back.

"I still don't like you."

"Noted. See you at seven am tomorrow?"

"Fine."

"Okay, big smiles now, you guys. Pretend you just won gold." The photographer positions himself behind the camera and begins clicking away.

Mia moves the snowboard in her hands around in a few different positions. "Oh, and don't worry, I'll try not to show you up out there tomorrow."

"Please, you'll be thanking me once I teach you a new thing or two."

She laughs.

I smile at her cockiness, realizing that I miss the banter between us.

The shutter of the camera clicks away as we smile on.

"Perfect," the photographer says. "The camera loves you two together. You look like you belong together."

Clearly the old saying, "The camera doesn't lie" is completely bogus.

CHAPTER EIGHT

The air is crisp, the sun yet to warm up the mountains of Utah. The new fallen snow crunches under my boots as I head to the snowmobile to take me to my halfpipe. After I attach my board to the snowmobile, I sit down and wait.

Fifteen minutes later, I'm still waiting and no sign of Mia, but people are waking up to make their way onto the slopes.

"Fuck this." I throw away my empty cup of coffee and Mia's still full one.

Roaring the snowmobile to life, I speed up the hill and over to my halfpipe. It's not that secluded, but I'm not one to kick a gift horse in the mouth.

"You've got to be shittin' me." I speed up the hill of the slope, kill the engine of the snowmobile and watch Mia fly up each side of the halfpipe, her body twisting and twirling in the air.

It's hard to know if she got her love of riding from Brandon or not. The whole following your big brother around town, or in her case up and down the slopes is the norm for most families. Brandon's no longer able to go to the Winter Classics, but his baby sister is the top female prospect to claim gold in the halfpipe.

She does the double cork she's been able to do for the past three years and falls into the airbag. She's too in her head. If she could get out of it and add to that trick she'd be unstoppable.

A minute or so later, she crawls out of the inflatable bag at the end of the halfpipe, two helpers grabbing her board for her. I wait at the top while she hops on a snowmobile. When it reaches the top, she hops off and thanks the guy who drove her up here.

"Morning," I nod.

She takes off her goggles and shoots me a dangerous smile. A smile that could make me grab her and push her up against a tree, kissing her until she forgot why she hates me, and why a piece of me hates myself every time I look at her.

"You're late," she says, and I grit my teeth but don't bother responding with the reason why. "I hope you don't mind, I woke up early." She glances behind her to the driver of the snowmobile and the two people at the bottom watching our interaction with curiosity. "I just thought—"

I rise to my feet, towering over her. "No problem. I offered it up, glad you're taking advantage."

Grabbing my board, I wish I wouldn't have called off my own team today. I'd thought it would just be the two of us and I'm not sure why I'm bothered that it's not.

"Well, your turn," she says and I watch as she runs ChapStick across her full lips. The way she purses them out a bit makes me want to find out what flavor she uses—with my tongue.

"I'm still setting up, you go ahead."

"Great." With her board under her arm, she heads the

last few steps to the drop in of the halfpipe before strapping herself to the board.

I wait, this time up on the hill, watching her do the same shit she just did a second ago.

Strapping on my helmet and my goggles when my turn comes, I let the music lead me. I mix up stunts I've been trying to perfect. Allow the freedom of flow to rule my tricks. Then I try the one trick I'm only ready to land in the airbag and a pillow of comfort catches my fall that would have been on my head had I tried it without.

The snowmobile guy rides me back up the hill, which is nice of him guy since he's only supposed to be here for Mia. She waits for me instead of heading down right after.

"Are you planning to do that at the Winter Classics?"

"We'll see." I shrug. "I'm not sure it will be ready."

She nods. "Is that your order of tricks?" I can't pinpoint what it is about her voice. Intrigue, but something else, maybe self-confidence.

"Nah, I freestyle it until the last few weeks and then coach and I will decide on the order. I tried to just do the same order time and time again, but I got bored with it and I think I lost my flare."

She nods, staring down at the halfpipe, her teeth biting down on her lip.

I lean in close over her shoulder. "You wanna know what I think?"

She cringes, stepping away from me. "I'm sure you'll tell me anyway."

"You play it too safe."

"Who asked you?" She straps both her feet on her board.

"Do one trick that you don't normally try into the airbag."

Without responding, she places her earbud in and slides down to the starting point.

Still stubborn as a fucking cat.

Her board slides down into the halfpipe and she does the same old shit.

Knowing she doesn't give a crap what my opinion is, I head down right after her.

And that's our first hour. Her dropping in, me dropping in right after. No conversation, no talking, just two athletes doing what they do best.

Then after a particularly challenging run, I find her waiting for me again at the top of the pipe, her goggles resting on her helmet, her teeth biting down on her bottom lip again. The snowmobile driver speeds back down the hill, picking up the two other teammates and they disappear, leaving us alone. I tense, getting the feeling that this is more than just break time.

"Hey," I say, placing my board in the snow and taking off my gloves.

"Can we talk for a second?" she asks.

I sit down on the snow. "Sure." My stomach clenches, prepared for a conversation like this since I found out we were going to be thrown together.

"Can we call a truce?"

My tense shoulders relax a bit. Not at all what I was expecting.

She picks up a handful of snow, pats it into a ball and throws, shockingly not at my face, but as far as she can behind her.

"I don't hate you, Mia, so I don't really need a truce."

She nods, her eyes concentrating on her mitten-covered hands piling the snow into another ball.

"Well, I hate you... at least I did."

"Mia?" She looks up, those brown eyes so similar to her brother's focusing in on me. "I get it. I'd hate me, too. We don't have to be best friends. You can use my pipe as often as you like without me even here. I don't care about that."

"What am I missing?" she asks, raising a brow.

"What do you mean?"

"Never mind." She shakes her head, second-guessing whatever it was she was going to say. We're both silent for a minute before she spits out, "I play it safe because I'm scared."

Shit, I should've kept my mouth shut, but it's hard when I see the talent she has wasted in simple tricks she perfected over a year ago.

"I know," I say softly.

"Aren't you? I mean you were there, you saw it."

Now it's me diverting eye contact and playing with the snow. I've avoided talking about that night with any of the Salters for four years. I'm not sure I can handle it.

"Yeah, but I love it. I'm myself out there and not all up in my head. It's like an itch I can't ever fully scratch. It took me a long time to realize that if I fear it, I'll never be successful."

"My parents aren't exactly thrilled about me continuing in Brandon's footsteps. He tries to explain the pull to them, but they aren't listening."

"If you didn't snowboard, what would you do?" I ask the tough question I had to ask myself. Is this worth losing it all?

"Nothing." She shrugs. "I love it, but I miss the adrenalin rush, you know? The feeling when you nail a trick you've been trying for months. You're right that I play it safe because I don't want the *I told you so* from my family should I slam."

"Then get up on there, and try any trick you want and land in the airbag."

She looks up from the snow in her hands, her eyes glowing with excitement.

"It's safe. Just see how it feels."

For a second, the silence around us feels oppressive and I second guess pushing her. Maybe she's not ready, but she surprises me when she stands and straps herself to the board with a short nod.

Without a word, she dips into the pipe, doing her run of the mill tricks until her final one when she tries a triple cork. She lands in the airbag, but she was close to nailing it.

Since the snowmobile isn't down there anymore, I hop on the one I rode up on and meet her at the bottom to bring her back up.

"How did it feel?" I ask, waiting for her to hop on.

She holds her board in her lap, smiling over at me. "Awesome. I want to do it again."

"Then we'll do it again."

I race us up the hill and for the rest of the day, she tries to nail the triple cork. For the first time in over four years, I laughed with a Salter and I'd be lying if I said it didn't make me feel both good and...undeserving.

CHAPTER NINE

I walk into the meeting room in the ski lodge pumped for the day. Today we're doing the Kids Day Out program, where we talk to underprivileged kids before they spend the day out on the slopes.

I always look forward to these...nothing can beat the look on the kid's faces when something you say to them clicks, or when they discover for themselves that they have a natural aptitude for the sport. It's like I've helped to open up a world of possibilities for them.

"Here you go." Candice shoves the bag full of hats for the kids into my arms then scurries off to talk to the program director before I can thank her.

I slide into the chair next to Mia who has a cup of tea sitting by her row of markers. As always, she has that faint smell of honey. I can't help but think that it's not normal to notice this. I mean, I can't remember thinking about what a girl smelled like ever before.

"Good morning," I say.

"Morning." She leans back in her chair. A pair of skin-tight leggings adorn her legs and she's wearing a sweatshirt with the logo of one of her sponsors on it. She's killing the endorsements, that's for sure.

"So, what's the drill?" she asks. "Just sign anything they bring up?" I think this is her first time doing anything like this.

"First we give speeches."

She cringes.

"It's not that bad. Usually the kids are all in awe, their mouths hanging open, that I'm not sure they even hear anything. Speak from the heart and you'll be fine."

"No one told me there was a speech. I would've prepared."

I sip my coffee as the kids begin to file into the room. Boys are whispering and pointing to me. "It's Grady Kale," I overhear a few of them say.

"You'll be fine. Just convey your love of the sport. How hard you worked to get here. That sort of thing."

She nods, but her face pales and for such a confident female. I never would've thought a room full of kids would intimidate her.

The manager of the program comes over to introduce herself. "Hello, I'm Georgie." She holds out her hand, her eyes locked on mine for a few extra seconds. She's wearing leggings, boots, and a long sweater that hangs open revealing a shirt that reads, Icing Isn't Just for Cupcakes.

"Grady." I take her hand. "Nice shirt."

She looks down as though she forgot what she was wearing and then smiles. "Thanks." Her hand extends to Mia and they shake hands.

"Mia." She smiles at Georgie, but it doesn't hold its usual friendliness.

"Can I tell you how excited I am to have you speak to the girls? We've been sharing stories this entire week about your journey to the Winter Classics. The triumphs you've had to overcome."

Mia's cheek flush the softest shade of pink. "I wish I was better dressed." The two of us look at her, but I'm pretty sure I'm the only one who has their blood flow being redirected to between their legs.

"You're dressed fine as you are. You're a snowboarder, that's what they expect." Georgie's known Mia for two minutes and can calm her down whereas I've known her her entire life and my words did nothing.

"Well, thank you."

Georgie smiles between both of us and then turns to face the group of kids that are now seated in front of us, legs swinging under their chairs, eyes poised expectantly in our direction.

"And here I thought she was more interested in you," Mia whispers, choking down her laugh.

"Well, she clearly prefers what you have to offer."

"Okay boys and girls, as many of you know, behind me is gold medalist, Grady Kale, and Winter Classics competitor, Mia Salter. Let's give them a warm welcome and thank them for having us here!"

Georgie steps aside, clapping on while her eyes are focused in on Mia from the side of the room now. Seems someone might have a crush on my sidekick.

"You go first." I nudge her on the leg with my pointer finger.

She shakes her head.

"No. You," she whispers.

"You want to go after the master?" I ask her and she rolls her eyes in a playful way, but says nothing. "Suit yourself, but you'll have a lot to live up to."

She giggles and I'm starting to like the sound of her happiness more than I should.

I stand and round the table, sitting down on it. My own legs swinging in the same fashion as all the kids.

"Like Miss Georgie said, I'm Grady Kale. I've been snowboarding since I was younger than all of you."

I talk a while longer, but hands are raised in the air before I give my full spiel. I prefer answering their questions to listening to myself talk so I call on the red-haired boy in the front row.

"Is the metal heavy around your neck?"

I shrug one shoulder. "It's kind of heavy, but you don't really notice it because of all the adrenaline running through your system when you're standing up there."

"Are you two boyfriend and girlfriend?" a blonde girl with pink-framed glasses asked.

I swear all the kids inch forward waiting for me to respond.

"No." I look over my shoulder to Mia, who raises her eyebrows.

"But my mommy said…"

Miss Georgie steps up to the girl and kneels down in front of her. "Katie, remember we talked about that? We're not to ask personal questions."

Katie leans closer and whispers loudly for all to hear, "My mom told me to ask."

I chuckle under my breath.

"I know, but we're here for them to tell us how they came to become snowboarders."

"My mommy says that Mia would be crazy to not want him. That he's so hot she's surprised the snow doesn't melt under his board."

Mia giggles behind me and I shake my head. "Looks like you have a fan out there," she mumbles.

"Why don't we hear about what they hope for in the upcoming Winter Classics?" Miss Georgie suggests.

"Yeah, Grady is going to win gold," the red-haired kid says.

I jump down and fist bump him. "Definitely."

"No, Matt Peterson will." The kid behind him kicks the other little boy's chair.

"Nuh-uh, Grady's gonna win."

"Now, now boys." Miss Georgie has to step in once again.

"Matt is a great rider, too. He'll definitely be a challenge for me." What I don't say is that I'll still beat him.

"How fast do you go down?" a kid near the back calls out.

"Pretty fast. The faster I go, the higher I get off the half-pipe." I slide back on the table. "How many of you ski or snowboard?"

A few kids raise their hands.

"They're all going out after this. A lesson on the bunny hill," Miss Georgie says.

I clap my hands. "Great. Can I join?"

All the kids' eyes widen. This is the reason I do this.

"Um." Candice steps forward from the side, her finger up in the air. "You and Mia have to do the promo shoot for that sponsor..."

I stare blankly at her. Does she want to tell these kids no?

Looking chagrined, she steps back until she hits the wall.

I return my attention to the kids in front of me. "Is anyone scared?"

A few kids look away. No one is gutsy enough to raise their hand.

"Let me tell you a story then."

"Were you scared your first time?" The red-haired kid who might be my biggest fan but did look away when I asked, seems eager for me to tell him some feel-good story about conquering my own fears.

I have fears that these kids wouldn't even understand yet.

"No." I look over my shoulder at Mia. "I was always a 'do it now and ask how later' kind of kid. Whatever my friends did, I did without really thinking of the consequences. Which did land me in the hospital a time or two and I don't recommend that for you guys."

They laugh although it's really not funny. I may have learned to play by the rules a bit to keep my career going, but challenge me, and I'm not one to ever tap out. Which can lead to disastrous results...

"This story is about a young girl. She had these two braids that were always uneven with a crooked line down the middle."

The kids laugh and I hear Mia scoff, which only spurs me to go on further.

"She begged for a board. Her parents said she was too young and asked why she didn't want to play with Barbies or dolls."

"She didn't love Barbies?" one girl asks, sharing a look with another girl.

"Nope. She didn't much care for makeup or anything girly. Her brother was a snowboarder and she wanted to be one, too."

The blonde-haired girl with glasses looks to Mia with a

knowing smile. She's a smart cookie and obviously has done her research on our story.

"Did they ever buy her one?" another girl in the back asks.

"They did, for her birthday. Her brother being a pretty cool older brother agreed to take her out the next day, show her a few tricks, so she went to bed that night with her board."

"In her bed?" the same girl with the Barbie question asks, eyes wide and again she looks at her friend.

"Yep. Probably hugging and kissing it like it was a boy."

"Okay, let's not exaggerate." Mia stands and slides to the front of the room, joining me on the table.

"The next day her brother and his friend took her up the ski lift which took a lot of convincing. We each took an arm and plopped her down between us."

"The chairlift can be intimidating at first," Mia says.

"Getting her off proved just as hard as she fell twice, but we finally got her situated, strapped into her board, standing on top of the smallest hill besides the bunny hill because she," I raise my hands and do air quotes around the last bit, "didn't need to warm up with babies."

I take my chances, glancing to Mia who is shaking her head in disapproval at my story. If I had to guess though, the gleam in her eyes makes me think she secretly enjoys that I remember.

"Did she go down?" the red-haired kid asks.

I nod. "After a lot of convincing and holding both my hand and her brother's halfway down. It took her the entire day to go down by herself, but she did it."

"Really? Does she still ride?" the Barbie girl asks.

"She does, and you know what?"

They all stare up at me.

"She's sitting right next to me."

"I knew it!" the red-haired boy screams, his two hands clapping.

"It was you?" a child in the middle row asks Mia.

She nods, knocking her shoulder into me. "I think Grady may have embellished the story a tad, but I pumped myself up for weeks and I thought I was ready. But standing at the top of the mountain is intimidating. It's okay to admit you're scared, but try to push through it because you might discover something great. Something that will change your life. I can't imagine my life without snowboarding now."

"Mia should be an inspiration to all of you. Sometimes fear can be your biggest motivator." I look to my left only to be caught by surprise.

Mia's staring back at me. Her mouth hanging open in surprise and her eyes holding softness I haven't seen directed my way in over four years.

Maybe it would've been better if I acted like I didn't remember.

CHAPTER TEN

"Hats for everyone." I pass out the hats with my name and sponsor's logos on them to each kid as some grab the towrope to head for the top of the bunny hill. It's about half and half, skis to snowboard ratio.

"Grady, Gasoline is expecting you." Candice approaches me, her teeth chattering since she's missing her ski jacket.

"Tell them I'll be there shortly. Have them start with Mia." I glance back and forth between my agent and the kids, enjoying the smiles on their faces as they take their hats from me.

"I think the girls need their own apparel," Mia says, joining us. She grabs the towrope, taking off my hat from one of the girl's heads and replacing it with one of her own.

"What? Did you go to the shop and buy all your stuff?"

She looks over her shoulder at me, a conniving smile crosses her lips. "I can't let them all look up to you."

"Great. My two biggest clients right now and they're both playing babysitter instead of making the people who pay them happy." Candice stomps off.

Cries echo out from behind me and I turn to find Mia squatting down in front of Barbie girl (who I now know is Katie). The two are in deep conversation, Mia's hands on the little girl's shoulders, and from how many times Katie's mittened hand has run under her eyes, I'm guessing tears are involved.

"Katie is a scaredy cat," the kid who thinks so highly of Matt Peterson yells out and grabs the towrope.

I grab it right after him, my board sliding up the hill as we start up the incline.

"Where are the others?" he asks me over his shoulder. His arm tucked around the rope.

"Hey buddy, you need to hold the rope with your hand."

Ignoring my advice, he says, "I get why they give us you because they're probably giving you a bunch of money to talk to us, but where's Matt or the other snowboarders?"

I reach forward lifting his arm off the rope and placing his hand on it the right way. "Grip it tight and hold on, otherwise it will tear your jacket apart."

He grabs a hold with both hands, but he's struggling and since he's a tad on the bigger side, it's probably making it harder.

"You have to be worried about Matt. My brother told me that if he would've nailed his landing last week he would have been number one."

I inwardly roll my eyes then notice the stuffing from his jacket spilling out because he's trying everything in his power to keep a hold of the towrope.

"I told you it'd ruin your jacket." Moving up behind him, I change the placement of his hands again. "I've got you in case you can't hold on. We're almost there."

"My mom is going to kill me!" He inspects his ripped jacket. "It's lasted my two older brothers."

"It's okay, I'm sure she'll understand."

"She won't." His shit-talking persona is long gone as his voice cracks.

Finally, we reach the end of the towrope and an instructor helps the kid away from the area, so there isn't a pile of kids at the top of the hill.

Miss Georgie slides over on her skis sticking her poles in the snow. "What's the matter, Ryan?...Oh." Her hand reaches to the torn underarm of his jacket. "It's okay. You know what? We have some jackets back at the community building. Your mom will understand, these things happen."

He hiccups a breath, and I glance over to the towrope to find another kid about to hyperventilate. Katie holds Mia's hand looking unsure of herself as they start to tip their boards down the hill.

Katie's eyes are closed and Mia's smiling down at her directing her with her voice about what to do. It's a touching scene and shows how patient and encouraging she can be. Two qualities not immediately associated with snowboarding's leading lady.

"Grady." A hand touches my arm, pulling me away from admiring the scene with Mia.

I blink. "Yeah?"

Georgie is putting her mittens on. "Will you take Ryan?"

I strap in my other foot. "Sure." I hold up my hands and the two of us ride, inch by painful inch down the hill. Ryan is smiling again, the problem with his coat forgotten as he finds himself living in the moment while the powder and wind rush past his face. Now that I think of it, he reminds me a little of me when I was young.

"THAT WAS SO MUCH FUN." Mia bounces in step next to me as we head to the Gasoline campaign. "That's so much better than boring interviews and promo photography."

"Yeah, it's pretty cool. Hey, I'll meet you up there."

"Are you bribing those kids with more stuff?" she asks with a smirk, walking backward away from me.

With my hand on the door of the store, I laugh. "Nope."

The heater vent rushes down on me when I step through the door and I unzip my jacket.

"Can I help you?" A woman follows me as I head right to the boy's jackets.

"I'm going to take this." I hand the woman the first black jacket I could find that looked about the right size.

Her eyes widen, recognizing me I assume, but she smiles, happy to help. Following her to the register, I pay for the jacket and head back outside.

As long as Mia is with Gasoline, I have time to deliver it before Miss Georgie heads back, but when I step out of the store, a smiling brunette is waiting for me, arms crossed over her chest.

"I knew it. Grady Kale has a heart." All her straight white teeth are on display, so I know she's not being snarky.

"Keep that between us, okay?" I wink and then jog down to the bunny hill, sliding through small openings of skiers and snowboarders on their way to the slopes. A couple of minutes later, I reach the group.

Miss Georgie is counting heads and Ryan is still wearing his ruined jacket as he laughs with a circle of boys.

"Hey, Ryan," I say and all the kids turn around. I toss

the jacket in his direction, it flies through the air, and he catches it before it falls to the ground.

The little kid's brown eyes inspect it and then he looks up at me. "Wh—"

"Bribery. Who's your favorite now?" I smile, and Miss Georgie stops her counting to witness the exchange.

"Definitely you." His voice low and unsure, wondering if he should accept it.

"Nah." I wink over to him. "If I win gold though, I want a fan letter, okay?"

All the boy's mouths are slightly ajar, their heads shifting from me to Ryan and back.

"Thanks," he mumbles.

"That was very kind of you," Miss Georgie says, her hand on my shoulder.

I point to Ryan. "Keep your hands on that towline and your armpits away from it, okay?" He nods and I look around at the rest of the kids. "See you guys next time." After a few fist bumps and high fives, I walk away.

I'm only a few steps back on the path toward the room Gasoline rented, when Mia pushes off the side of the building, walking in line with me. She knocks my shoulder and I get we called a truce, but I never expected her to be this friendly with me.

"That was a very nice thing to do." She sing-songs, glancing my way.

"Was I supposed to let the kid freeze?"

"I don't think he would have frozen."

"He's not used to it out here." I continue to make excuses, so she doesn't get the wrong idea. I'm not deserving of her thinking I'm a nice guy. I'm her enemy and she should remember that and stay far away. Except, I like that she's warming up to me.

What the hell is wrong with me?

"Oh good," Candice stops in front of us on the path, heaving for a breath.

"You need boots, Candice. And not leather ones." Mia shakes her head at the knee-high fashion boots Candace is wearing.

"I'll remember that for when we're in Korea." She sucks in another breath. "Listen, Gasoline is ready so let's talk while we walk." She swivels around and leads the way, Mia and I following behind.

"What's up?" I ask.

"Tomorrow I need the two of you to head to Colorado. I have to get back to L.A. because my little sister is getting married. Can you believe it? I told her the timing wasn't good, but no, her selfish side is being indignant, so why not put everyone's life on hold so she can marry the world's biggest douche—"

"Why Colorado?" Mia interrupts her rant, inching forward.

"The entire team is going to be there for a big shoot, but they want you two there a day early since you have more to get done." She opens the door to the resort and I grab the handle holding it open for both of them.

"Don't they realize we have to train?" Mia asks. "I was just working on—"

Candice raises her hand in the air. "Relax. They're blocking off the halfpipe at night for team use. So, your day will be filled, but you guys can train at night."

"I love night riding," I remark and Mia shoots me a dirty look. "What?" I shrug.

"We have Grady's pipe here, it's easier—"

"Please don't become all high and mighty on me. This comes with the territory. Go be some snow bunny if you don't want to be bothered with their demands. Do I need to remind you—"

"No, I get it." Mia rolls her eyes, unzipping her coat and walking through the doors to the room Gasoline has set-up in.

Candice stops me before I go in. "One more thing."

"Why is there always one more thing with you?" I raise a questioning brow.

Candice smirks. "You're both flying there together and staying in a lodge. Break the news to princess, okay?"

"Whoa, whoa, whoa." I raise my hand in the air. "Why?"

"The entire team will be staying at the lodge, but the first night it's just you two. Some team building nonsense."

She walks away and my eyes wander over the room when I enter. There are cameras placed all around, a white cloth draped up with lights shining on it, a table full of junk food, and a coffee station. My eyes land on Mia, already in the makeup chair.

A whole night under one roof—just the two of us. One of us might not survive.

CHAPTER ELEVEN

I thought Mia and I were on our way to a semi-cordial relationship, but other than a grumpy good morning, she's had her earbuds in the entire flight. She demanded to wheel her own bag from the baggage carousel outside to the driver the resort sent. I understand why she's mad about this team building, and we have a lot of training to do, but we have no control.

I eye her next to me on the bench of the pickup truck that's taking us up to the lodge. She's a control freak. I should have pegged her for one—the way she's religious about her schedule, the way she always has one of those green shakes in her hand.

It takes a few minutes before she realizes I'm staring at her. She plucks an earbud out of her ear and shoots me the dirty look she's perfected over the last couple weeks.

"What?"

"You're pissed because you're not in control."

Her eyes narrow. "I'm mad because I need to train and we're going to be fighting for a chance to do that here."

"Maybe we can work something out."

I lean forward, tapping our driver on the shoulder. The lady, who looks like she could kick my ass any day of the week, looks at me in the rearview mirror. "Do you know if they'd let us rent the halfpipe for an hour or two, so it would only be us?"

"Can't say for sure, but probably not."

"Figures," Mia sneers as she returns her attention to the scenery outside the window.

"Really? I could make it worth their while." I don't usually throw my name or my money around, but I was just making headway on my own trick, so I get where Mia is coming from.

"You're throwing your clout around?" Mia asks.

The woman's attention darts to her in the rearview mirror. "It's not about the money," she says. "The halfpipe will likely be closed in a little more than an hour."

"What?" Mia sits up, both earbuds hanging down now. "It's beautiful out there."

We each look out the truck windows to see the sun shining down. It couldn't be better boarding conditions.

"The wind. It's supposed to come up this afternoon. It's the first round for the weekend. Didn't anyone in your group look at the weather?" She shakes her head in disbelief.

We probably take for granted that it's skiing weather, but Mia and I both know the wind is a factor when it comes to flipping in the air.

"Can you take us back to the airport?" Mia asks and I swear she's seconds away from leaning over the seat and grabbing the steering wheel to take control.

"I could take you to Denver, but then I'd have a lot of people mad at me." She laughs like she's the headliner at some comedy gig. "Because you'll never get out of the local airport now."

Mia's hand lands on her leg and she balls it into a fist. "You can't be serious. All of this in the span of a couple hours?" She looks at me with her mouth ajar like 'aren't you going to take care of this.'

"The airport was running smoothly when we left." I offer my bit of advice and if the driver's bored eyes in the mirror are my response, I clearly don't know shit about their airport or the minute-by-minute weather changes.

"That was then. Weather can change fast, Mr. Kale. Just like life. This wasn't forecasted a couple days ago, otherwise I'm sure they wouldn't allow the two top prospects for gold to be stranded somewhere."

The truck slides on the road and Mia's hand reaches out, grabbing hold of my thigh. My dick jumps in my pants despite the circumstances, but she lets go as soon as she realizes what she's done.

"Stranded?" Mia reacts like she just told us a meteor is about to land on Earth.

I understand her reaction, the two of us having to survive in a log cabin by ourselves for however long we're stuck here is not exactly going to let us sail into the Winter Classics on good terms. The girl has finally spoken more than two words to me. This much togetherness and she'll probably murder me in my sleep.

"Probably by morning would be my guess."

Mia's gaze zeros in on me, her eyes widening as though we know each other well enough to have an unspoken language. "Then take us to Denver," she demands.

The truck wheels slide again. "Should have put on the chains," the driver mumbles.

I glance out the window the sun still shining down, but

white snow is whipping across the ground now, visibility dwindling the further we head up the road.

I shift my gaze back to Mia and then out the windshield again. This time we do share a common look that says *fuck, we're stuck together.*

She closes her eyes and leans her head back on the seat, inhaling a deep breath, her lips now a tight line.

A few minutes later, the driver parks the truck outside the lodge. A lodge way too big for the two of us, which might be good because maybe we can stay on separate levels and not have to speak a word to one another.

Mia's out of the truck immediately, grabbing her suitcase from the back and a little like a toddler, stomping her way up to the lodge.

"Normally I'd show you around, but I better get back before you have a third guest for the night." The driver laughs, handing me the keys to the place.

"Thanks."

"The fridge is stocked with what was requested. There's firewood on the south end of the cabin. I wouldn't be trying to work the outside hot tub in the coming days."

"No worries on that front," I mumble, pushing the thought of Mia's curves in a bikini as far from my mind as possible.

"If you need anything, call the main number, but from the looks of it, we might not be able to get to you. You're a big strong guy and that girl of yours seems like she can hold her own, so I'm not worried." She nods, heading back to the driver's side of the truck.

The vehicle circles around and heads down the hill. I look up to the cabin where Mia's arms are wrapped around herself, her angry expression directed at me.

Jogging up the snow-covered pathway with my suitcase in hand, I step under the overhang of the porch. "Sorry."

She says nothing as I unlock and open the door. "Would you like me to carry you over the threshold?"

There's zero amusement from her, not even an upturn of the corner of her lips. Grabbing hold of her suitcase, she walks into the house.

Great, this is gonna be a blast.

CHAPTER TWELVE

I'm sprawled out on the sectional, the television remote in my hand, the signal going in and out. My eyelids are fading and for the first time in years, I might actually grab a nap. That is until my phone rings with the blaring music of Dax's ringtone.

His name flashes across the screen and my thumb hovers. A nap sounds better than whatever Dax has to say. Then again, it'd be nice to talk to someone who actually *wants* to speak to me.

"What's up?" I answer.

"I heard you and Little Salty are tucked away in a cabin all cozy. You tap that yet?" He laughs, certain that would never happen.

"Let me warp back to two thousand and five and I'll let you know." I click off the remote. Senseless.

"That should show you how much of a gentleman I am, I don't even know the current slang for banging."

I press speaker, sit up on the couch and grab a magazine from the coffee table and start flipping through it. "Gentleman, you are not."

"Hey, I've been dry so far this year. Saving myself for the village in Korea." He laughs.

"You grab that economy size box of domes from Costco?"

I stop on an article about Matt Peterson. A picture of him so far in the air I can only hope it's Photoshop's doing.

"Hell no, you know they supply them for us. Or do you? You never blow off any tension with a good lay, Rogue."

I do, I just don't advertise it like my buddy does.

"Why are you calling again?" I ask.

"Just checking to make sure you're alive is all." Beckett's laugh sounds in the background. Of course Dax isn't alone.

"I hid all the knives," I deadpan.

"Watch her and make sure you watch your six," Beckett says.

"No worries, I'll die of boredom first. She hasn't come out of her room all afternoon."

I slide to the back of the couch, my feet resting on the coffee table. At least if I was with them, we'd be playing cards or doing some other bullshit to pass the time. Dax would probably be boarding off the roof.

"You're better off then," Dax says.

"I don't know, death by boredom is slow and painful. If she jabs me in the heart, it's quick and over with." I rest my head on the back of the couch, my eyes shutting, that nap sounding better and better.

"You underestimate me. I'd make it as slow and painful as possible."

My head snaps up and sure enough Mia's standing in the kitchen, a mug in her hands.

"Is that Little Salty?" Dax asks. "Hey, Lil' Salty. You're going to play nice, right?"

"I always play nice, Soups." She starts heating water in the kettle on the stove. "Hoff, you there, too?"

"Hey, Mia...how'd you guess?" Beckett asks.

"Because the three of you do everything together."

"Not everything," I mumble.

"If you want us all, Mia, you just have to ask," Dax says and laughs.

"I think she might only want one of us." Beckett chimes in.

I roll my eyes. The guy wasn't even around back when I got razzed about her following me around.

"Don't flatter yourselves." Mia grabs a tea bag from the cabinet.

She's in pajama pants, a long sleeve tee with a big puffy pink sweater. I'm not sure what's bigger, her sweater or her socks. She glances at her phone on the counter.

"I have references I can give you, Mia. Guaranteed stellar performance," Dax says.

I shake my head at Dax's idiocy.

"We better go hit the slopes. You two can just...hit it." Beckett does his monster laugh.

"Screw off." My gaze focuses in on Mia, while she grabs her cup and rounds the couch to sit on the opposite side of me.

"Oh, and FYI, our flight is canceled, so, use the manners your mothers taught you. I don't wanna be haunted with a murder scene when I finally get there." Dax laughs loudly and the line clicks off.

I bend forward and click off the phone. "You're going to join me?"

She sips her tea, her brown eyes staring at me through the steam. "I did about everything I could to stay away. Turns out I'm way too efficient and organized."

"Not a bad thing."

"Television?" she asks, her gaze moving from me to the remote.

"No signal."

She pulls a blanket from the edge of the couch, cuddling into the softness. "Do you think they have cards?"

"What are you thinking?"

She smiles, her expression suggesting that I should know, which I do.

"You sure?"

She nods still believing she'll beat me.

"Your funeral." I stand up and head over to the drawers on the nearby table and jackpot, every type of card imaginable. "Pinnacle?" I hold up the cards. "Bridge." I hold up that pack. "Euchre." Then I pluck out the regular poker cards. "Gin Rummy anyone?"

She places her tea on the table, rubbing her hands together. "Bring them to Mama."

I toss them on the table and she misses no time in pulling them out and shuffling the deck using her fancy bridge method.

Instead of joining her right away, I head to the kitchen, grabbing a bag of pretzels and a bottle of water. I can't wait until I can really spoil my diet, but that day is way too far into the future to think too much about now.

I jump over the edge of the couch and land on the cushion two away from her.

"Pretzels?" she asks.

I shrug. "Could be worse." I pry the bag open and I hold it out to her. "Want some?"

She picks up the bag and holds it up to her nose, inhaling the scent and then passing it back to me.

"No?"

She starts dealing the cards while shaking her head. "I'll eat the entire bag."

Not about to beg her, I keep them on my side of the table, popping one at a time in my mouth.

She sips her tea as we start discarding and picking up cards. Then when I think she's about to lay down three cards, she leans over and tucks her hand into the bag and sneaks a pretzel.

I say nothing as she chews, her eyes concentrating on the cards on the table.

For the first time in I don't know how long, there's a comfortable silence between us.

CHAPTER THIRTEEN

"And that's two." Mia lays down all her cards. "Gin Rummy, baby." She does a little shimmy with her ass on the couch.

"Three out of five?" I ask, pulling all the cards my way to start shuffling.

She grabs a handful of pretzels and leans back on the couch. "Don't say anything." She points a twisted pretzel my way.

"Hey, I've said nothing." I hold up my hands and then go back to shuffling. "You want a beer to chase them?"

Ding, a pretzel hits my head. I pick it up and throw it at her. She throws two more at me, and they fall to my chest. Picking it up from my lap, I pop it into my mouth and eat it.

I pass out the cards and she sits up straighter, poised and ready to win her third in a row. She's lucky I'm not that competitive with her.

"So, that truce we agreed on?" I ask. She peeks up from her cards but says nothing. "You still gave me attitude earlier..."

Again, she glances at me then takes a card, discarding one of hers. "I'm just mad."

"I get it, it's hard to be told to sit when we've been working so hard to get here and we're only months away from Winter Classics. But you need to pace yourself anyway. Otherwise, you'll peak too early." I discard a card, arranging the rest in sets. "I'm sure coach has told you this."

"That's not what's hard." Her hand reaches for a card and then slides it into the bunch fanned out in her hands.

I tilt my head. "What is? If you don't mind me asking?"

She stacks her cards and lays them facedown on the table, picking up her mug. When her eyes meet mine, my stomach tightens.

We're finally going to have the conversation.

"It's hard to be around you." Her words come out in a rush, but the pained look on her face suggests they were hard to put out there.

I lay my cards down, standing and rounding the couch, pushing my hand through my hair.

"We should just talk about it." She swivels to watch me as I head to the kitchen.

I open the fridge and hide my head inside for a second, acting like I'm perusing what it has to offer. Really, I'm being a chicken shit because more than four years later, I'm still not prepared for this.

"You to clear the air." The words catch in my throat. I don't want to screw this up.

"Grady," her voice holds a plea.

Finally, fucking the diet up completely, I grab a beer and shut the fridge door. With my back to the counter, I twist the cap off, flip it around in my free hand while gulping a good amount down my throat.

She watches me and knowing that I've been trying to

outrun this moment for years and that it's time to be a man and own up to my sins, I round the back of the sectional and take my seat.

"I understand why you hate me. I'm sorry for what I did. If I could take it back, I would. I shouldn't have—"

"Disappeared," she cuts in. "No, you shouldn't have. You were his best friend. How could you?" The pain in her voice lances through me like a scalpel.

I gulp down another chug of the beer, buying myself some time.

"I had to go to the Winter Classics." Brandon's accident occurred weeks before and it was our dream. A dream we shared. Maybe it was selfish of me to go, but when you reach that level it's not just about you anymore. There are a lot of people who helped you get there and are counting on you to perform—coaches, sponsors, therapists, teammates.

"I know that. You think I don't understand how hard that decision was for you?" She twists the edge of her sweater between her fingers. "Brandon gives you the benefit. He always says you did what you had to do, but you could've done both. You should have visited him after. You abandoned him at the worst possible time in his life. How could you?"

"I know." The beer bottle slides along the coffee table when I set it down. "I know," I whisper, my voice having lost some of the fight.

Silence occupies the room and I wish I didn't want to hold her so bad right now—like I did the night of the accident. I remember how much comfort it brought both of us.

"Why didn't you?" The soft plea in her voice makes my chest tight and it's hard to push the breath in and out of my lungs.

"Because—"

"What, Grady? What was more important than your best friend fighting for his life? Even today he fights to have a normal life. He lost everything you gained and you still stay away. You deserted us."

The way she used the word *us* and not *him* doesn't escape my notice.

I stand to my feet without making eye contact, and end up back in front of the fridge, with my hand on another cold bottle of beer.

"Are you going to drink yourself stupid?"

She's right behind me now, her signature scent of honey lingering around us.

God, I hate what that smell does to me. Makes me want things I can't and shouldn't want. This whole fucking situation makes me so angry.

"I deserted him, not you." The fridge door shuts at the same moment her eyelids do. "You're upset because you've always had some sort of crush on me. You feel as though I left you behind, too."

One tear slips from her closed eye, but when they open, you'd think she had some magical power to will the wetness away because her pupils are angry and piercing right through me.

"That's not true. Did I have some crush on you? Yes. Congratulations you figured out what everyone else already knew back then. But after you left Brandon behind and found your success, you became about as attractive as an ogre to me."

She slices me right back with her words.

Game on.

"Really?"

Her eyes narrow.

"So, if I stripped off my shirt right now, your mouth

wouldn't water? How about if I caged you against the counter, pressed my hard dick between your legs, your body wouldn't react?"

She swallows, her eyes not leaving mine.

Brave girl.

"Try it and I'll spit in your face."

I shake my head, taking one step forward. "You still want me and guess what?" She remains silent and I step into her. She straightens her back, her hands clutching the counter's edge. I run my thumb along her hairline, down the side of her face. "I've noticed you these past weeks. Your body." My eyes dip to her chest, noticing the rise and fall of her rapid breaths. "And I want you, too."

We stand there, my dick growing more uncomfortable every second. I think I finally found something to keep me busy while we're stranded.

"I'm sorry, Mia. You were young and my best friend's little sister. Our closeness those weeks after his accident...I couldn't do it. I never meant to hurt any of you though. I just..." How do I tell her about the guilt that racks me, that I blame myself every day for what happened to Brandon?

A glop of spit lands on my right cheek.

I step back, swiping away the saliva from my skin.

"I told you, I'd spit on you." She slides away from me, but I grab her wrist.

"Whatever this is, isn't going away."

"I wouldn't want you if you were the last dick on Earth." She wiggles out of my hold and heads down the hall back to her retreat.

CHAPTER FOURTEEN

I'm lying in bed, thinking about what I did. What I said and how I let my dick speak for me when I should've told her I was sorry and that I was an ass and my reasons for distancing myself from the Salter family have nothing to do with any of them.

Eventually, frustration over the spinning wheels in my head has me throwing the covers aside. I'm sick of tossing and turning, stuck in the darkness of my own head. Grabbing my T-shirt from earlier, I throw it over my chest and open my door. Seconds later I find myself two doors down across from my own room, my knuckles gliding down the wood. I shake my head. Not a good idea and head to the great room instead.

I flip on the outside light on the porch, leaning my shoulder on the window and watch the snowfall pile up on the deck. The branches on the trees are covered with white powder. I can't help it. My first thought is of boarding on white powder and my second is of who I'd want to share the experience with.

Mia comes to mind, and I inwardly reprimand myself

for allowing her name to pop to mind. What the hell am I thinking? If I have sex with her, there's no going back. There's no *that was great, on to the next*, or *this was awesome, glad we worked each other out of our systems*. I couldn't do that to her—I've already caused her family so much pain.

I close my eyes and literally shake my head in an effort to gain my sense back. We're friends again which is more than we've been in years and that's where it needs to end. I have no choice but to forget the sway of her hips, the swell of her breasts, the curves of her body…

Jesus, I shift my stance and adjust myself.

"You're right."

I spin around, finding Mia in her pajama pants from earlier, but now she's wearing a tight tank top that doesn't hide the fact she's braless. My eyes take in her hard nipples until she quickly pulls her hoodie closed over her chest.

"I don't get the pleasure of hearing you say that very often," I say, trying to keep the mood light.

She steps forward, one deliberate and slow step in front of the other, ending up on the opposite side of the large framed window, watching the snow come down.

"Yes, so savor it." The sweetness of her voice has my head turning in her direction. A smile creases her lips. "I *was* hurt when you pulled away from Brandon. *I* felt abandoned."

I nod. "I'm sorry. I couldn't handle it all. I had to get back to competition, Brandon was unconscious and we were getting closer…nothing was making sense."

"It was probably for the best. I might've embarrassed myself even more." Her long dark hair shakes back and forth as she turns her face to hide it from me.

Stepping forward, my finger pulls back the strands of

her hair, tucking it behind her ear.

"You were young. Seventeen and we were twenty-one. Everything in our lives was chaotic and uncertain."

She glances at me from the corner of her eyes, a smile upturning her lips. "Maybe I just wanted what I couldn't have."

My vision dips again, and my hand clenches from the pure want running through my veins.

"Maybe." She's millimeters from me and I watch her staring out into the darkness. "I'm sorry, Mia."

She nods, turning, her back to the window. Her eyes close and slowly open. "I'm kind of exhausted from hating you."

"So, my punishment has been suspended." I bend down so our eyes are on the same level.

"Yeah, I suppose so." She rubs her face along the edge of her sweatshirt and shoots me a look that hits me right in the heart.

"Then let's celebrate." I grab her hand and pull her along with me.

"That's doesn't mean I'm going to sleep with you."

I glance over my shoulder, winking but saying nothing. We're in agreement there. "We're going to celebrate with ice cream sundaes."

"I can't," she says, but doesn't fight me and I pat the counter in the kitchen.

"Up."

"Grady," she sighs, but does as I ask.

I dig out the vanilla, cookie dough, and chocolate ice cream out of the freezer and put them on the counter. "Please, we aren't going anywhere for a few days."

I find chocolate sauce and cherries, but sadly no whipped cream. What a letdown.

"Fine. A small one." She indicates a size with her hand, but that's not going to happen.

"And we can finish our three out of five Gin Rummy contest."

"Why bother, I'll totally beat you." She tucks her hands under her thighs and watches me scoop the ice cream.

Ten minutes later, she's got a bowl of cookie dough with chocolate syrup and five cherries while I chose to stick with chocolate ice cream doused in chocolate sauce.

With bowl in hand, I prop up on the opposite counter so we're sitting facing one another, our eyes meeting every bite or two. "You're really nailing the trick. I think you're ready without the airbag."

A nervous look crosses her face. "Nah."

"Can I ask you a question?"

She peeks up from watching her spoon move the ice cream around. "Sure."

"Why do you play it safe? I mean...I get the Brandon thing."

I'm unsure how to bring the subject up, especially since it's me, but Mia was once fiercely set on upping the bar.

She continues to swirl her spoon around the bowl, her gaze never lifting. "I guess so, I mean it definitely set me back a little, but..."

Her attention finally moves from her ice cream and lands on me, hesitancy saturating her features.

"What?" I ask when she doesn't continue.

"It's just the pressure," she says.

"I get pressure."

"Not really the press and their expectations, it's my family. If something were to happen to me..." She eats a heaping spoonful of ice cream.

With my own spoon twirling and mixing the ice

cream/chocolate sauce blend, I make the eye contact with her. "I get it. There has to be a lot of pressure to play it safe."

"After the accident, my mom wanted me to quit. She even reached out to your mom and asked her to help with this campaign to lower the walls of the halfpipe."

"I remember." I don't want the walls lowered, but how could anyone blame a mom whose son was in a coma for over a month and won't ever be able to fulfill his dreams, from trying?

She nods. "My dad and Brandon are the ones who convinced her to let me continue. She reluctantly agreed, but I don't drop in that pipe without remembering that my mom's heart will shatter if something happens to me."

"Oh, Mia." My own heart drops to the pit of my stomach. How could I not realize that? Of course, she's playing it safe for her family's sake. That's Mia. Everyone else before herself...always.

She shakes her head. "Don't. You've really helped me, Grady, and I appreciate you pushing me. I think it's too painful for Brandon to help me and most of my trainers don't even try to up my tricks because I'm winning now, but that won't always be the case. Plus, it's been fun with you, makes me remember why I love it." A shy smile forms on her mouth and she takes a small spoon of ice cream.

"I think I'm fucked up because after Brandon's accident, I tried harder tricks."

She raises her eyebrows. "Would you like to psychoanalyze you now?"

"Definitely, not." We sit in silence for a while, the only sound is the scraping of our spoons against the bowls. Words are begging to come out of my mouth, but I just can't get them out. My eyes catch hers from across the small room. "Mia, you should be so fucking proud of yourself. You're an awesome snowboarder and I wouldn't push you if I didn't think you could handle it."

Her cheeks flame, a subdued shade like the cherries in her bowl. "Thank you." She takes another spoonful of her sundae and ends up getting some sauce at the corner of her lips.

I motion with my hand where she should swipe. Her tongue snakes out of her mouth to lick it off, but she can't reach it.

"Nope. Here." I point to where and her hand reaches up on the other side. "No." I laugh, placing my bowl down and jumping off the counter.

The minute my feet hit the hardwood floor something shifts in the air. I was only going over to help her get the chocolate sauce off, but suddenly, her tits with their erect peaks are screaming for my attention and I'm wondering if she's bare under her pajama pants, too.

Her tongue continues to explore her mouth in a failed attempt to clean herself up and now it's her lips stealing all of my attention.

I slide my thumb along the edge of her lips, and the chocolate smears across my skin. I hold my thumb out to her, but her eyes study it and then raise up to meet mine. Knowing she's not going to, I suck the chocolate sauce off my thumb as she watches me with interest.

She sucks in a short breath and seems to hold it.

I step closer and to my surprise her legs open for me. I pull her forward until she's hanging off the counter, my hands threading through her hair. Without thinking about the repercussions, my lips land on hers and I'm transported to Miaville, where I know one kiss won't be enough and I hope to enjoy a good, long stay.

CHAPTER FIFTEEN

She doesn't pull away from my advance, instead one hand fists my T-shirt to keep me in place. I push my hands into her long, brown hair as I try to figure out how I've lived this long without ever kissing her. Her tongue is cool from the ice cream and runs along mine. Mia isn't one to shy away from what she wants and the fact she wants me, or at the very least my lips in this moment has my heart fluttering like some lovesick fool from the movies.

Her legs clench around my thighs, locking me to her. An internal debate runs in my head.

Take your time, savor the moment, there's too much baggage between us for this to happen a second time.

But already I know—one taste will never be enough.

Her hand releases my shirt and I draw my hands away, letting her hair fall back down as our lips slow to a close. I draw back and eye her beautiful, swollen red lips.

"I'm sorry," I say, immediately regretting making it even more weird between us.

"Don't be." She lets a small giggle escape. "I've dreamed of that moment most of my adolescence."

We both smile and though my dick is screaming for me to go back for more, something stops me.

"Grady?"

My gaze flies up to her.

"I'm not looking for a ring or some declaration of everlasting love." She tilts her head, studying my reaction.

My heart sputters. Is she saying what I think she is?

"I want you," I whisper, my forehead falling to rest on hers. My hands disobey my brain's instructions of hands-off, and instead I grab the strings of her sweatshirt, wrapping them around my fingers.

"Then have me."

When silence bears down heavily on us, her hands move up to cradle my face, forcing me to look directly at her. "Don't overthink this, just go with it."

My hands push up under her sweatshirt, sliding it off her shoulders. I need to taste her and so I cast small kisses up her bare shoulder and down her collarbone. She falls back on her hands, allowing my teeth to grab a hold of her nipple through her thin tank top.

Mia's breath leaves her in a rush. "Oh." Her body freezes for a moment and then I suck her entire nipple into my mouth, my tongue twirling the hard nub around. My other hand glides up her ribcage and pulls the tank top down on one side, revealing a perfect, perky tit with a kissable nipple.

I move over to her exposed tit and take it into my mouth roughly. The first taste only makes me hungrier, and I slide a hand down the front of her pajama pants, finding her bare and slick.

"Oh, please, Grady," she pants, her back arching, offering me even more of her.

My cock grows more rigid and throbs with an unbearable ache, needing to get inside of her. I lift her up off the counter, heading toward the great room and lower her to the couch. Grabbing the edges of her pajama pants, I slide them down her legs.

Her perfect bare pussy glistens with wetness as my prize for unwrapping what will be my sweetest present ever. My dick is standing at full salute in my pajama pants and she notices, licking her lips when she does.

I wish Mia would stay down so I could examine every inch I'm about to taste, but Mia always does what she wants. She gets up on her knees, her hand sliding up the front of my pajama pants, fisting my dick through the thin fabric. Jesus, her hands release any remaining restraint I had.

I reach out, pulling the hem of her tank top up and over her head. She has to take her hands off my dick momentarily, but lucky me—she uses a switching hands technique and now I know for certain that mine isn't the first dick she's touched.

Rest assured, I'll make sure it's the one she remembers most.

"God, you're gorgeous." I take in all of her. Her olive skin flawless from top to bottom. Her dark hair spilling over her shoulders, almost touching her nipples. Her doe eyes that silently beg for me to take her.

She scoots closer to me, hooking her fingers on either side of my pants and sliding them up and over my erection until I step out of them.

"Impressive." She stares at my cock with a hungry look and I say a quick thank you for being blessed between the legs.

"Not even in the same realm as you." I take in her puckered nipples, my mouth salivating to latch on like some preteen kid who's looking at his first porno mag.

Her cheeks flush and she rises to her feet, taking my shirt with her until it's stripped off my body, joining our other clothes. Then without warning, she hops up and I catch her. We're skin to skin. Her erect nipples press into my chest and the wetness between her legs coats my stomach. The tip of my dick is so close to her pussy that it's almost painful to resist its siren call.

"Condom?" I ask, panting.

"Definitely."

A short burst of excitement races through me at the thought that if she's not on the pill or have one of those things inside of her, she probably doesn't do this all the time. Maybe there are a few things I'll be the first person she experiences them with.

"My room then," I say and start walking with her still in my arms.

Her lips attach to mine, not that I'm complaining, this cabin is entirely too large when you have a gorgeous woman strapped like a koala bear to your body and a condom isn't within reach.

What seems like a lifetime later, I kick my door open and dispose of her on my bed. Oh, how I wish this was my actual bed at home, so I could mentally catalogue that picture for the remainder of my days.

She watches me as I go to my suitcase, grabbing a condom. I toss a few on the bed and start crawling toward her.

"Someone thinks a lot of himself," she says, glancing to her side.

With my hands on either side of her body, I laugh. "Sweetheart, you'll be begging for more."

She falls into laughter and gently pushes my shoulder. "You're so full of yourself."

"Get back to me afterward." My head dips down to her neck and she turns it to the side, giving me access.

Her fingers grip my shoulders, her nails digging into my flesh. The tip of my dick teases her entrance, and she starts to grind. If I'm not careful, I'm going to slip into her wetness and lose all rational thought.

"Now. Please." My tongue leaves the sweetness of her skin and I sit back on my legs, stripping one condom off the row and opening it up.

"You're so..." She stops and our eyes meet as I roll the condom over myself.

"What?"

"Just." For the first time, Mia's voice is tentative and I hate the fact she doesn't feel comfortable telling me what she's thinking. That's not like her.

Lowering my body on top of her, I flex my hips.

I brush her hair off her sweaty forehead. "Tell me."

"You're just really...good looking."

My eyebrows raise and she tucks her head into the crook of my neck, embarrassed.

"Well, thank you, you're really...cute." She slaps my back and I lean back, my hands cradling her face. "Relax. It's just me."

Her eyes fill with so much emotion I have a hard time processing it all.

"That's the problem." She swallows hard. "It's you."

I shake my head. "Just go with it." I throw her words back at her and she giggles until I swallow it down with my own mouth as I slowly slide into her.

Her hips rise off the mattress and her fingers tighten on my skin while a moan catches in her throat. Not stopping the kiss, I wait until I'm fully seated, then pause for a moment so she can get used to me.

Instantly she grinds, circling her hips and I take that as my sign she's ready for more. Our lips devour one another's, our tongues battling for dominance as I thrust in and out of her. Sometime later she pushes on my shoulder and I follow her lead and flip onto my back so she's straddling me.

"Thatta girl," I urge the sexual kitten on.

I slide right back in without any resistance, my hands cupping her tits, my fingers tweaking her nipples. My cock is deep inside her and she keeps making little circles on top of me, spurring me to heights I'm unsure I can control. Needing to slow the pace, my hands reluctantly leave her breasts to mold to her hips where I rock her back and forth on me.

She falls forward, grabbing the edge of my headboard, her nipple right in front of my mouth. Taking the opportunity, I suck it in past my lips, twirling it with my tongue, and it's her undoing as she rides up and down on my cock.

"Shit, Grady." My name comes out as a plea for more. Her orgasm overtakes her body, she clenches around me, her body trembling as my cock pulses inside of her.

My fingers dig into her hips, making sure she doesn't move an inch. When they finally loosen, her body falls on top of me. I trace the arch of her sweaty back as her labored breaths create the sweetest melody in my ear.

"Did I live up to the hype?" I ask.

Her giggles vibrate along my skin. Eventually, she picks up her head and rests it on my chest. "Better." She winks.

I blink. For a moment, the resemblance to Brandon makes my gut twist and harden. Will I be responsible for bringing down two Salters?

CHAPTER SIXTEEN

"I'm gonna need you to ditch the clothes." My shoulder rests on the wall opposite the window I was staring out last night when Mia came to me. Only now I don't see the snow inches up on the window, or the weighted branches of trees, limbs about to snap from the piles of snow. I only see Mia, holding her cup of tea, her sweater wrapped tightly around her for warmth.

She glances over her shoulder, a smile that was never reserved for me until recently, graces her lips. "I wondered when you'd wake."

I walk toward her, wrapping my arms around her waist and burying my face in her neck. "Someone couldn't get enough of me last night." She elbows me in the gut, not hard enough to do any damage. "It's okay, I know I'm edible."

Her tea sprays all over the glass and she covers her mouth, laughing.

"What am I? The ugly stepsister?" She leaves my arms and heads over to the kitchen.

"You're definitely Cinderella." I take the wet paper

towel from her hands when she returns and clean the tea off the window.

"You already got me into your bed, you can lay off the sweet talk." She holds out her hand, but I bypass her to throw away the soaked-up towel. "And now you're cleaning up after me? Where's the real Grady Kale?" She takes her tea and sits on the couch, taking the remote off the table.

"You made me coffee?" I pour some into a mug and join her on the couch.

"Don't think you're special or anything, I was contemplating having a cup. Went for tea instead."

I plop down right next to her, grabbing her thigh and placing her leg over mine. Leaning over, I kiss her check. "Thank you."

She says nothing, but body language speaks volumes and the way she's tilted herself slightly away from me is like a megaphone in my ear.

I'm not sure where the girl that rode me like a bull at a rodeo is, or who the girl who had me licking chocolate sauce off her chest at three in the morning when we got hungry has disappeared to. I'm seeing a foreign side of Mia, a shy, timid side that I don't like.

"What's the deal?" I ask.

Dodging any eye contact, she sips her tea. "What are you talking about?"

"Why are you acting so different?"

She gives me a fleeting glance and then looks back to her cup of tea. "I'm not."

"You are."

She takes a deep breath, gives her head a shake and then curls up in the corner of the couch, her legs pressed to her chest. "What is this?" Her finger motions between the two of us.

"This?" I mimic her movement.

She rolls her eyes and places her teacup on the coffee table. "Us. Where do we stand now?"

I really try to fight the smile, but it breaks through because I might be surprised with this side of Mia, but I've changed my mind. I like it...a lot. Bending forward, I place my coffee cup next to hers.

"I was thinking we might as well take advantage of our time alone." I pick her up and plop her on my lap, my already hard cock pressing against her ass.

She wiggles, her hands planted on the back of the couch. "You know what I mean." This time her eyes are locked on mine. Goodbye shy girl and here's the Mia I know. Direct and upfront.

"Listen." My hands hold her face in them and she leans into my right palm. I ignore the way that made my stomach do something funny. It could totally just be too much chocolate sauce last night. "I don't know where this is going to go, but last night was not a one-night stand. At least not for me. I'd never do that to you, given our past. The only thing I know is that I liked last night." I flex my hips up, circling my pelvis. "And I like this."

Finally, her teeth emerge and all the tension in her face vanishes. "Me, too."

"So, can we stop talking for a bit?"

She rocks against me and my hands fall to her hips. "Definitely."

Leaning down to me, her lips land on mine and I get lost in Miaville again. I'm not quite sure I'll ever grow tired of roaming her streets—whether it means being out for a leisurely Sunday walk or racing through town in a sports car.

My hands move, sliding up the hem of her tank top, my

fingers poised and ready to tweak her nipples when her body starts sliding off me, falling down between my open legs.

I watch her, the way she pulls my pajama pants up and over my rigid length, her eyes on my cock. The way her tongue slides out and licks her lips. Peeking up to me through her eyelashes, our gazes lock as she takes me in her mouth.

"Fuck." My hands move to her hair, tightening in her dark strands and my ass slides to the edge of the couch, opening my legs farther to give her more room.

Her head twists and turns around my dick until she takes all of me and then she works her way back up—she's slow and almost painfully arousing and all I can think of is how I want to fill her mouth.

My eyes won't leave her handiwork and my dick grows harder the longer she's down there. Last night she teased me briefly, but I know she's down there to finish the job this time and there's nothing sexier than watching a girl who enjoys blowing you.

The more she sucks and the more the sound of slurping saliva echoes through the room, the harder it becomes to hold back. Suddenly, my head feels like it weighs thirty pounds and it collapses to the back of the cushion, as I rock my hips up.

She fists me, pumping up and down at the same speed as her mouth is sucking the life out of me.

"Fuck, Mia. Your mouth..."

She lets out a moan or whimper, I'm not even sure because her other hand cradles my balls and it's game over. They tighten up inside of me and though I try my best to hold back, I lose it.

"I'm coming." I use the last of my energy to try and pry her off my dick.

She shakes her head, not stopping and I explode in her mouth. Her eyes meet mine and she swallows—holy fuck, she swallows!—licks her lips, pulls back and smiles. I think she just put my dick out of commission for a while, but I crave the taste of her.

She happily obliges when I reach for her wrist and pull her up so she's straddling me once more, but this time I flip her onto her back and she yelps.

"Let me repay you the favor."

The smile that overtakes her face tells me this is another area in our lives where Mia and I are on the same page.

CHAPTER SEVENTEEN

W e're on our second full day at the cabin and the signal on the television is finally working. Mia is snuggled into my side sleeping, her hand on my stomach, her breathing tickling my neck.

I'm watching a military movie hoping to wash off the three previous hours she forced me to watch Thirteen Reasons Why.

The good guys end up in a gunfight with the bad guys and the surround sound is so fucking awesome in this place I literally feel like I'm in the middle of the town they're destroying.

The noise must be disruptive to Mia because her eyes flutter open and she slides up my body enough that the blanket drops to her waist, exposing her naked tits. Just like that, I'm a boy scout because my dick is tenting the blanket. I'm fairly sure my dick is about to fall off, but unless something changes, we're screwed because I only have two condoms left, which if I do the math, only gives us until dinner and then we're shit outta luck. Maybe Pinterest can tell us how to MacGyver our own condoms.

Without warning a body jumps up over the back of the couch beside me, and onto the coffee table.

I'm busy processing what's happening until I notice Dax staring at Mia, his jaw practically to the floor.

"Fuck!" I scramble to move and cover Mia.

She wakes up in the process, her eyes blinking and closing and blinking open again. Somewhere on her journey to consciousness, she realizes what just happened. We're outed and Dax might have seen her breasts. Her eyes narrow on me like this is my fucking fault.

"You fucker. Brandon's really going to want to kick your ass now." Dax points at Mia and I cringe knowing whatever is coming out of that mouth next will not be good. "Great tits, Mia. Perfect ten," he says, all ten of his fingers spread out in the air.

CHAPTER EIGHTEEN

"I take it the airport is open?" I say between gritted teeth, trying to adjust the blanket, but with only one Dax either sees my dick or all of Mia.

"Yep. You better hurry and get dressed. They're all on their way up here. Lucky for you, Beckett and I hitched a ride first."

I stand, my two hands covering my dick. "Let's go." I look at Mia and nod in the direction of the bedrooms.

She says nothing, instead laughing at me trying to cover myself. I grab the magazine off the coffee table and use one hand to cover my junk and hold the magazine over my ass.

"If you only need one hand to cover your cock, man..." Dax's face cringes and I look around to find Beckett, but he's nowhere.

"Please, you probably only need a Post-it note." Mia's come back brings a smile to my face. She's sticking up for me.

"More like a whole pack sweetheart." Dax winks at her.

She rolls her eyes, wrapping her blanket all the way around her and heading out of the room.

Dax jumps up off the table, his gaze set on the kitchen, no doubt to rummage through whatever we have. "Hey," he says right when I'm about to follow Mia.

"What?" I glance down at myself to remind him once again, I'm standing here naked holding my dick in my hand.

"What's the deal? Are you two a...couple?"

"Can we talk about his later? Maybe when I don't have to worry about a bunch of people coming in here seeing me naked?"

He grabs a bag of chips, turns around opening the top. "That driver lady told me we only had vegetables or some shit. She's a ball crusher, huh?"

"I'll be back." I start walking toward my room.

"You do that pretty boy. Oh, and Rogue?"

I huff a breath, turning around. "Yeah?"

"Nice ass." He winks.

I roll my eyes, circling back to my room.

"I didn't want you to think I only noticed Mia's spectacular physique." Dax's laugh slowly drifts away as he makes his way through the house to check out the place.

"Shit." I walk into my room, shutting and locking the door.

My eyes case the room, and until now I hadn't realized what we'd done.

I pick up the lamp that's sitting on its side, thankfully not broken. Bundling all the sheets and the comforter, I roll them into a pile on my bed then grab all the clothes up off the floor, and shove them in a drawer.

All anyone will think now is that I'm a slob.

I sit on the edge of the bed and I can't help the thought that creeps in. What will it be like between Mia and me now that other people are around? Then the reality of Dax's words hit me. We may not be friends anymore, but Brandon *is* going to want to kick my ass.

———

TWO HOURS later and I've yet to see Mia come out of her room. The guys are getting ready to hit the slopes with the hopes that it's not too crowded yet since the storm only ended earlier in the day.

I knock on her door and the faint sound of feet shuffling on the floor sounds through. My lips are already turning up when the doorknob twists, but when the door springs open, it's not Mia.

It's Demi—the auburn-haired skier with so many freckles you could play connect the dots, pursing her lips. If she were an emoji, her eyes would have question marks in them.

"Mia here?"

"Sorry, we intruded on you guys." She opens the door wider, inviting me to step through.

"We need to practice anyway," I mumble, heading into the room, finding Skylar on the bed, her attention fixed on me over top of the Powder Magazine she's reading. Mia's Gasoline endorsement ad is on the back where she has an orange mustache.

"Grady Kale." Skylar's voice insinuates she hasn't seen me a long time, but I get her tone.

"Skylar," I deadpan. "Where's Mia?"

Her snow boots are out, her pants and jacket strewn across the bed. Of course she's going out, too.

"In the bathroom. Getting all your cooties off her." Demi waggles her perfect reddish-brown eyebrows at me.

"What are your intentions with her?" Skylar tosses the

magazine in front of her crossed legs and piles her long dark hair on top of her head in a messy bun.

"Intentions?"

"Yeah. Like is this just a little action on the side for you?" Demi steps up close, her face serious.

I'm getting the feeling I inadvertently stepped into the lion's den with two very protective mamas.

I shake my head. "That's between Mia and myself."

Skylar stands, cornering me on the opposite side. "We don't want our friend to get hurt." Her finger runs down the zipper of my coat like she's flirting with me.

I pick up her hand and drop it to her side. "I'll be back." I step away from them and the bathroom door opens. Mia's in her yoga pants and a long sleeve shirt that fits like a second skin on her body.

My dick twitches and I thank the Lord I'm in snow pants. These two beside me might have cut it off if they noticed.

"Hey." I glance warily at her friends. "We're heading out." I head nod in the direction of the slopes.

She smiles and begins braiding her hair. Damn. She looks pretty either way, but I love it loose and wild.

"What do you say, girls?" Mia asks.

They step up shoulder to shoulder with me. "We were having a conversation with Grady." Demi raises her eyebrows like she's still waiting for me to answer her question.

"ROGUE!" Beckett's voice roars through the three-story cabin.

"Oh, Beckett's going to save your ass, is he?" Skylar says.

I hear him coming down the hall, humming one of the shitty nineties songs he loves so much.

"In here, Beck," Skylar says next to me. "If only you were more like him."

I shoot her an annoyed look, rolling my eyes. What's that supposed to mean? More like Beckett? What, afraid to seal the deal and go for what I want? Why the hell Skylar and Beckett haven't gotten together yet I have no idea. They're attached at the fucking hip. Even in the offseason, they get together for birthdays and shit. *Friends* my ass.

"There you are." Beckett's bright, blue eyes take in the room, spotting Skylar immediately. His smile grows. "Hey. When did you get in?"

Skylar leaves my side, her arms already extended when they meet halfway, hugging one another. "We got in an hour or so after you."

"We're heading out to the hills, wanna join?" Beckett asks her and she looks over to Demi.

"Is jackass going to be there?" Demi's face droops.

Each of us laugh because her and Dax have a sordid past from the last Winter Classics and Demi can't seem to let what happened between them go.

"Demi," Mia shakes her head. "Grady and Beckett are going. Since when does Dax not follow them like a lost puppy?"

"Hey now." Dax stands in the doorway, obviously eavesdropping. His gaze zooms in on Demi, raking over her body. "Demi." He nods and winks at her.

She wraps her arms around herself. "Dax." Her tone suggesting she just said hello to Satan himself.

"Why are we all in here? Let's go!" Dax's voice booms and he claps his gloved hands in front of himself.

Mia walks past me and the scent of honey—which I now realize is her lotion—wafts around me, putting my body on alert.

"We were just asking Grady what his intentions are." Skylar crosses her arms over her chest, jutting out her hip.

Beckett's two dimples emerge as he laughs, leaning his arm on her shoulder, waiting for an answer from me.

"Let my boy be." Dax busts past Beckett, knocking his shoulder. "He pleads the fifth."

Demi's eyes shoot little daggers into the back of Dax's head. "Most people are like the company they keep."

My eyebrows crinkle. "I'm not like Dax."

Mia's behind me now so I can't see her expression or what she's thinking about this whole interrogation I'm suffering through.

"Really?" Demi doesn't appear to be sold on my upstanding character.

"Beckett isn't like Dax either," Skylar chimes in and as suspected, this little mobster role-playing scene was Demi's idea.

"Thanks." Beckett winks at Skylar and her attention flies to his lips.

It's like two blind mice with those two.

"It wasn't my fault that you..." Dax is ready to hammer it down on Demi but we need to keep this cordial. We have two more nights to be together as a group and I'm not about to spend it refereeing Demi and Dax when I could be fucking Mia.

"Yeah guys, we're still figuring this out, so cool it, okay?" Mia comes to my side with just her snow pants on, her tits so tightly tucked into her shirt, her nipples can't be missed.

I smile down at her and swing my arm around her shoulders. "I'm just going to say this and then it's end of the conversation, okay?"

Dax's eyes are fixed on Demi and Beckett is smiling toward me, the two other girls' heads are tilted, waiting for me to reassure them they won't be having a devastated, heartbroken friend in a few weeks' time.

Dipping Mia, she yelps, but I swallow it down as I kiss her hard, fierce, and hopefully answer every last question of whether she's just a good-time girl to me. Her hands fist my jacket, keeping me pulled to her and if all the assholes weren't in the room, I'd suggest hitting her before hitting the slopes.

Instead, I prop her back up, leaving her breathless with rosy red lips and cheeks. That lazy pleasure-filled smile covers her face. I hope that smile never leaves her face when it comes to me.

"There. Now let's go," I say like it's settled.

The other four mill around the room, all mumbling about public affection and they would have taken my word, but after they file out and Mia pulls her jacket on, I cage her to the wall by her bedroom door.

"Tonight, I want you in my bed." I bend down and kiss her neck.

"Maybe I want you in mine." There's a lightness in her tone, which I love because I haven't heard her use it with me in years.

"I don't care whose bed we're in, as long as we're in it together."

She grabs my jacket, pulling me close. "Me either."

I kiss her and grab her hand, leading her to the great room, but she stops me.

"What?" I turn around to see what the hold up is.

She bites her lip. "Um..."

"You having doubts?"

"No." She shakes her head. "It's just, Brandon called."

It's something I know I have to address, I was just hoping for more time before I had to. "And?"

"He'll be there when we get to Korea. One of the TV stations asked him to be a guest announcer for the Classics."

I try to keep my face neutral as if I'm not concerned what he might think of me and his sister.

"Did you tell him about us?"

She focuses her gaze on something over my shoulder. "Not yet. I didn't know..."

I step into her, gripping her hand tightly in mine. I give her a light peck on the lips, hoping to ease her anxiety. "I'll take care of it."

She grins, seemingly feeling better about it, but my own stomach feels like I ate a bomb and it's ticking, ticking waiting for Brandon to cut the wrong wire.

CHAPTER NINETEEN

The airplane turbulence rumbles the queasiness in my stomach further. This flight to Korea feels like it's never going to end.

Mia is fast asleep, her head lying on the pillow by the window, earbuds in her ears, an American flag blanket pulled up to her chin.

The seatbelt sign dings and I pick up my whiskey on the rocks, folding up the tray table. The entire plane is dark except for the glow of cell phones sprinkled throughout the rows of travelers. Dax is sprawled out over three seats in the middle. Beckett looks over, raising his water to my drink as he studies video footage of his competition in the upcoming competition. Always the preparer. Skylar's head rests on his shoulder as she points to the iPad screen and murmurs something to him.

The chilled glass rests in the palm of my hand and my gaze once again lingers on Mia. I pull my phone from my sweatshirt, wondering how I explain what's happened between us to Brandon. Although, when we were younger the jokes never bothered him about Mia's crush on me. Like maybe he thought it'd be cool if I dated her. Our families were so close back then.

I felt Mia's tension rise when we boarded the plane and came that much closer to facing her brother. Which means what Brandon thought four years ago, may not be what he thinks now.

She moans softly and nestles into the pillow more, her tongue licking her lips. I rack my brain for a reason. To tell Brandon exactly how this all came about. How Mia and I went from hating to...I don't know what. Surrendering? What I do know is that I've been enjoying the hell out of her warm body next to mine at night. We've been training every day, but our energy's never too drained to get in another workout in the bedroom.

The plane dips again, a little more abrupt this time and Mia's eyes flutter. I admire her, the deep breath she inhales when she first wakes up, the way her eyes look around like she slept so deeply she may have forgotten where she was. Then her gaze lands on me and the corners of her lips tip up and as quick as a snap of a finger, I feel like I'm already standing on the center podium, leaning down to claim my gold medal.

"Hey." Her voice is soft and lulling. She sits up, a slight tilt of her head, pulling the earbuds out of her ears. "What's wrong?" Her gaze fixates on my drink for a second but returns back to my eyes.

"Nothing, just admiring how beautiful you are."

Her smile widens and my heart swells. And yeah, I know what a lame ass that makes me sound like, but there's no other way to describe this feeling.

"Hmm. You sound guilty or something."

I chuckle and then look around, quietly leaning forward and placing a kiss on her lips.

She welcomes my advance and then licks the seam of my lips. My hand slides around the back of her neck, pulling her toward me and I pour all my admiration for her into the slow rhythm of our tongues sliding against one another.

"Mmm," she coos as I close the kiss. "I love waking up to you."

I wrap my arm around her and she lifts up the seat separator, curling her legs up into her and letting her head fall to my shoulder.

"Sleep," I whisper.

She peers up at me, her fingers wisping along my five o'clock shadow. I see it, her acknowledgment of what it means that I'm awake on a plane at one in the morning with a whiskey in my hand. Like everything else in our past, we push it to the back burner because we know, like a timer on a bomb, its counting down on our happy bubble the closer we get to the Winter Classics. It won't just be us—my parents will be there, her parents, the press, and most of all, her brother—all to remind us how insane we are to think there can be something lasting between us.

Her breathing evens out almost immediately, her hand stuffed into the pocket of my sweatshirt. The seatbelt light goes off a few minutes later and the flight attendant comes by and I hand her my whiskey. Wrapping my arm around her shoulders, I let her honey scent intoxicate me because I'm going to enjoy our happy bubble while we still have it.

"I'M GOING to grab myself some kimchi," Dax says and rubs his stomach.

"You don't even know what that is," Demi quips and stomps on ahead.

"You should wait until after the competition," Beckett offers his advice as him and Skylar walk ahead of everyone.

Mia's hand is tucked in mine, and I think we're both eager to get to the villages although if we'd gotten together earlier, I would've tried to set us up in a hotel instead. I'd sleep a whole lot better with Mia as my roommate rather than Dax.

"Hell no, we're going out tonight." Dax turns around, moving his feet and dancing in place. "We're here, we made it, and we need to celebrate."

Mia and I share a look and she rolls her eyes.

"I'm fairly sure eating spicy cabbage isn't going to do wonders for your system," I say.

Dax falls in line with us. "Whatever, the gas alone will make my opponents pass out."

We all laugh, if only that were the case, every Winter Classics athlete would be heading for the kimchi.

"I'm sure they have it there, Dax," Mia says. "We have to catch the train."

I release my hand from Mia's, pulling her close, my arm swung over her shoulders. "I think maybe you were made for me."

She tiptoes up and kisses me on the cheek.

"You guys can be so boring sometimes," Dax moans.

I smack his stomach and he fakes hurt.

"Maybe that's why we're the best," Mia sing-songs.

I pick her up and swing her around. "Man, you really were made for me." I press my lips to hers and before either one of us thinks better of it, our tongues are swirling and our bodies heading to the pull to be closer together.

"You two totally deserve what you're about to get,"

Dax's sour voice is like background noise until I hear the clicks.

Snap.

Snap.

Snap.

I close the kiss, and Mia draws back, our lips only millimeters apart.

"Fuck," I whisper, having forgotten momentarily that the fact press would be nearby waiting our arrival.

"I guess we're coming out." She bites her lip.

Prepared to face the press, I set Mia back on her feet and grab hold of her hand. We both turn to start walking again, but those contagious smiles we've had plastered on our faces the last two weeks disappear when we see what—scratch that, *who*—is waiting for us.

"Mia?" the deep male voice asks.

Her hand leaves mine, walking a few steps ahead, rising on her tiptoes and wrapping her arms around her brother's neck. "Brandon!"

He holds her to him, but his eyes are focused on me over her shoulder, and from the looks of it, he just pulled out the pin of the grenade that's going to shatter the happy bubble we found ourselves in.

CHAPTER TWENTY

"No one told him before now?" Skylar asks me, sitting down beside with Beckett with a smoothie in hand.

"I wanted to do it face-to-face." I lean back against the bench of the train.

Mia's a few train cars up with Brandon, trying like hell to explain what's going on.

"Now's your chance," Beckett says, but his face clearly conveys that I'm up a creek without a paddle.

Dax plops down in the seat across the aisle. "Brandon looks good."

I nod.

"Yeah, maybe he's over the whole enemies thing with you two." Skylar glances at Beckett and they share the same hopeful look, but I'm sure that's not the case.

"You know what, I'm going to talk to him." Dax stands. "I'll clear the air and tell him how his sister is way too hot for you and she should probably go for me."

I roll my eyes. "Sit down."

"Don't you think someone should be going up there? I mean Mia shouldn't be defending your relationship all by herself, should she?" He raises his eyebrows at me and then sits back down.

"I'm impressed," Skylar smiles over at Dax.

"Did you think I was a complete asshole?" he asks impassively as if he just asked her the weather.

"Yes. Yes, I did," she says with an equally straight face.

"Chicks." He shakes his head, propping his feet up on the bench across from him and pulls out his phone. "Now, I don't want any drama ruining my concentration." He smiles up at me, places his earbuds in his ears and throws his sweatshirt hood up over his head.

"You know he's impersonating you, right?" Beckett asks.

"Yeah. Jackass."

"Heard you," Dax says.

"Jackass," I say again.

"Love you, too," he says so loud heads turn. "You sitting here the entire trip?" he asks and then leans back like he said nothing.

"I think the jackass has a point, Grady. If you really like Mia..." Skylar trails off.

I stand and place my hand on her shoulder. "I'll be back."

She smiles and glances at Beckett like I just announced I'm going to propose.

Not sure which train car they're in, I walk forward, my steps feeling like I'm walking through wet cement the farther I go. Passing by and fist pumping or waving to a few other athletes I know, I find them in the third car up. Mia is facing me and all I can see of Brandon is the back of his head. She's wiping tears off her cheeks and leaning forward. From the looks of it, they're arguing.

Fuck.

Her eyes catch mine and remain focused on me the

entire walk up the center aisle. Brandon turns, rolls his eyes, and then mumbles something to Mia.

"Hey," I say, my heart thumping like a bass drum in my chest and nausea casting a thin sheen of sweat over my skin. I'm not even this nervous when I'm competing.

Mia slides over, but I don't want her here when this conversation goes down. This is between Brandon and me.

"Mia, give us a minute?"

Her gaze swivels back and forth between the two of us.

"How about a please, asshole?" Brandon sneers.

I hold my hand out and she accepts my gesture, rising to her feet. Not wanting to throw more gasoline on the already burning inferno, I keep it platonic with her and don't kiss her the way that is starting to feel normal to me.

"Thanks," I murmur. She nods and I'm shocked she's allowed me to take control here without putting up a fight. "Everyone else is three cars back. Except Demi. I'm not sure where she is. Dax said something to piss her off and she went to sit on her own."

"Okay, I'll go join them."

I take Mia's spot across from Brandon. His challenging brown eyes aren't something foreign to me. We've been competitors our entire life. The only difference is that usually after a second or two a smile or a laugh would emerge, because we used to be friends, too.

"How are you?" I ask.

"Cut the bullshit." Brandon's death glare is like nothing I've seen before.

"Fine, I'm dating your sister and I don't plan on stopping just because you have a problem with it. Straightforward enough for you?"

He huffs. "Should've realized you'd take what you want and not give two shits about what anyone else thought."

"You said you didn't want any bullshit." I lean back into my seat, my hands gripping my knees.

"I want you to stay the fuck away from my sister."

"Sorry, not gonna happen."

Even I hate myself right now. What the fuck am I doing? I should be groveling to my former friend. Telling him how much I care for his sister, not playing this whole alpha pounding my chest gorilla shit.

He sits back, bringing his ankle to rest on his opposite knee. "Since I've been off the circuit, and a lot of my time is spent on my ass, I've had a lot of time to think. I don't hate you, Grady."

"Of course you do."

He shakes his head. "I don't. I get what you did, not coming by. I might've done the same thing. It was scary as shit and I know you, so I'd bet the farm that every time you're about the drop into the pipe, my accident flashes in your head."

My lungs constrict in my chest and I say nothing.

"You're scared that one false move and you're me, or worse. We've had friends who suffered a lot more than me. I can never snowboard competitively again unless I want to end up completely brain dead, but there are guys out there that didn't quit the first time. I'm proud of you, that you didn't quit."

His fingers strum along his leg, which I don't remember him ever doing before.

"But my sister, man, I can't in good faith be okay with this. You ran away from me because you were scared, so what's to say you'd stand by my sister's side if something happened? She's too good for you."

"I agree." I lean back in my bench seat, mimicking his sitting position. To anyone outside of our conversation they'd think we were talking about music or movies, not the fact that I'm screwing his sister. "She's way too good for me, but that doesn't change the fact she likes me and I like her."

"And what about after the Winter Classics?"

"We'll figure it out, me and her."

A hollow laugh rises out of his throat. "She's making a mistake."

"It's hers to make. "

His one foot falls to the floor with a thump and he leans forward. "Have you considered the fact that you could just be a crush? That once she knows who you really are, she'll realize that you're nothing more than a wannabe hotshot."

His shot hurts as intended, but I'm not ready to pull out my gun. At least not my big one.

"We both know I was going to win, whether you competed or not."

I don't really believe it, but like I'd say anything different in this scenario.

"You know I was better."

"Listen, I'm not gonna get into a pissing contest with you. I wanted to sit down and let you know I'm dating Mia and I'd appreciate you not giving her shit about it. She's got enough on her plate right now."

"I'll tell you what? I'm not going to lie and tell her I'm cool with it, but I won't make a huge deal out of it. She's an adult and she can do what she wants, but I can't say what will happen after Winter Classics."

I hold out my hand. "Deal."

He glances at my hand and for a second and I don't think he's going to shake it. Eventually, his hand slides into mine.

I pull out my phone, texting Mia to come back.

"I am glad you finally opened your eyes and saw how amazing Mia is," he says.

The accident must have brought them closer because the old Brandon never would have said that to me. Now I just need to make sure I don't fuck this up, but with my track record, that's easier said than done.

The excuse that Mia should spend time with her brother has rolled off my tongue more than it should in the past week. I've been on the halfpipe every moment I could, practicing because I have to nail these Winter Classics. I need to show Mia and everyone else in the Salter family, I am the best there is. I'm *not* second best.

"You need to calm the fuck down. You're going to injure yourself." Beckett sits next to me at the restaurant, giving me unwanted advice.

"I'm fine. Going out with you tonight. Thinking about training with you on slope style, practicing my tricks in the big air."

"Um...no." He flags the waitress down.

"Why not?"

"Because you're about to kill yourself. Relax, we have a week and a half before the competition starts, just master what you're already doing."

We hear some commotion and turn to find Matt Peterson walking in with his entourage. Half the restaurant points and screams his name.

"Fuck that guy's annoying," I grumble.

Beckett smiles over at me, popping the popcorn from the bowl on the table into his mouth.

"How the hell are you eating that shit?" I ask.

He shrugs. "Where's Mia?"

"She's with Brandon."

He nods slowly, piling another handful of popcorn into his mouth.

"Oh, look there's Mr. Self-Destructor." Dax slides into the chair next to Beckett.

I roll my eyes in response.

"What a fucktard, right?" Dax eyes Matt Peterson. "I mean, try earning something before you act like a damn rock star." His hand competes with Beckett's for popcorn.

The waitress sets what I know will be Beckett's one and only beer for today down.

"Me, too, thanks," Dax squints at her name tag. "Soo."

"Soonil," she clarifies.

"Is there a difference?" he asks.

Beckett shakes his head.

"Yes, there is." She gives him a fake smile.

"Then my bad. Beer please, Soonil," he pronounces every syllable of her name.

She spins on her heel and walks away.

"There's one that won't be sleeping with you," Beckett says, grabbing a bowl of popcorn from the empty table next to us.

"You can't share?" Dax asks.

"With you? No."

"You'll share with who knows how many other pee stained hands, but not Dax's?" I ask.

Dax truly looks offended.

"Considering how often he beats off, Dax's might not be pee."

"Hey now. That's just mean…I don't have to beat off. I have plenty of willing partners." He tosses a few kernels into his mouth.

"Bullshit," I cough out.

Soonil drops the beer off without saying a word or really stopping. "Thank you, Soonil," Dax screams out after her.

She doesn't deem him worthy of a response. She's probably right.

"Not all of us have a hot chick in our bed every night." Beckett eyes me.

"I think I'm going try Demi again this time around," Dax says and both our heads snap in his direction.

"That ship has sailed," I say.

"Not only sailed, I think the boat has been burned and sunk to the bottom of the ocean with no hope of being retrieved," Beckett adds, sipping his beer.

"Why? We had fun last Winter Classics." Dax throws popcorn up in the air, catching it in his mouth.

"You're really not that clueless, right?" I ask, sipping my energy drink.

Someone drops into the seat next to me.

"Rumor has it, my boyfriend has been training way too hard and not fulfilling his obligations to me." Mia tilts her head with a smile.

Her hair is thrown into a bun on top of her head, an ear warmer hanging around her neck and a jacket covering up the body I love to admire.

"Get him off the pipe, Mia," Beckett says. "He's going to hurt himself."

She grabs a piece of popcorn from Beckett's bowl and pops it into her mouth.

Not her, too.

"I agree. If he's not careful, I'll text Candice about it and she'll be on your ass, too, when she gets here."

I roll my eyes. My friends, my girlfriend, my coaches, and Candice? That might be more bitching than I can handle.

"He's been pushing me aside since we arrived." She pretends to narrow her eyes at me and I can't help but smile at her teasing.

"Take me home and I'll fulfill all your requests." I swing my arm around her shoulders and kiss her.

She pushes me back. "You have to woo me," she stands up, raising her eyebrows in a challenge.

"Yeah, see you guys. I have to go woo." I stand, pushing in my chair and following her out of the restaurant.

"You're leaving me with clueless here?" Beckett yells out.

"Fuck off," Dax says, but when I glance through the restaurant window, I find they already have two girls sitting across from them to take our place.

"So." She links her arm through mine. "What's going on with you?"

"Nothing." I shake my head.

She stops us outside the athlete's village where they have a path of ice sculptures depicting various sports on display.

"Bullshit, come on, Grady. Level with me."

It's cold and I pull her toward me, holding her with my hands locked behind her back.

"Nothing, let's go in and grab a handful of condoms on the way to my room."

"Eww, Dax walking in on us again? No thank you. My room."

"What about your roommate?"

A smile teases her lips. "She's already found love with a guy who does Skeleton."

"Skeleton? Are they boning?"

She stares at me for a minute. "Corny joke, babe."

I can't help but chuckle.

"If you want to work yourself to the bone, Rogue, work me with your bon-er," She grabs my jacket and pulls me forward while walking backward to the door of her building.

"Who has the corny jokes now?"

I follow her giggle right into her room.

I CRAWL BACK up the sheets, finding a very satisfied Mia attempting to catch her breath.

"Was that a bribe so I don't give you shit about your training?" she asks, leaning on her side, holding her head up with her hand.

I pull her on top of me, my hands pushing the hair back from her face. "No, that was a thank you for the blow job this morning."

She bats her eyelashes. "I aim to please."

"Well, that was a gold medal performance. Can I request another wakeup call tomorrow morning?"

Her head falls into the crook of my neck. She's clearly as tired as I am. I wonder what things will be like after our events are over? When we have a few months off.

"If you stay in bed until nine o'clock."

That's her little jab since I'm out at seven am every morning to be the first one to the pipe.

"Come with me tomorrow." I tickle her ribs and she

squirms in my arms, eventually falling over and placing her head on my chest.

"We'll see. Hey." She props her chin on my chest. "Come have lunch with me and Brandon tomorrow?"

My hand tucks a strand of hair behind her ear. "How has he been about us?"

She smiles. "Great. Doesn't say much. Whatever you said must have appeased him. Thank you." She slides up and kisses my lips, her bare breasts pushed against my hard chest.

I say nothing because who knows what will happen after the Winter Classics and because the truth is that I miss my friendship with Brandon.

"The Gasoline party should be interesting...with all of our family there."

Our sponsor has decided to throw a party for their athletes and families the weekend before the competition begins. Which means my parents and the Salters will all be under one roof. Add on the fact that Mia and I are together, and whether or not Gasoline arranged for fireworks at the party, I know there will be some.

"It'll be fine. They only want us to be happy and we are."

I lean forward and kiss her forehead. *My sweet, naive girl.*

I roll on top of her, my lips casting soft kisses along her neck and collarbone. "Do you have enough energy?"

She pulls my head down by the back of my neck. "For you...always."

Our lips crash together and my hand is already stretching out for a condom on the side table.

So far, I've found that an intense orgasm does wonders to push away reality.

CHAPTER TWENTY-TWO

"You can do this," I whisper in Mia's ear at the top of the pipe.

She nods, not making direct eye contact with me.

Her board slides to the starting position and I watch from the top, other snowboarders starting to wake-up and test out the course we'll be on next week. A line is starting to form, which means we have limited time. Which sucks.

She dips down, her motions fluid as always. Coming up the one side she grabs huge air.

"Man, is that Mia Salter?" the girl behind me asks. Based on her coat and her accent, I'm fairly sure she's from Italy.

"It is." My tone that of a proud boyfriend.

"She looks great."

Mia's onto her last trick and this is where she needs to land what her and her coach have been working on. Without any hesitation, her board leaves the edge of the pipe with more air than I've seen her get on the final trick.

"Shit," the Italian girl's defeated voice says behind me.

"Way to go, baby," I say mostly to myself as I prepare to get to the edge to congratulate her.

She raises her hands from the bottom of the pipe, her head turned in my direction. All I want to do is race down there and pick her up and tell her how amazing she is.

I slide down to the starting spot, placing my earbuds in. Like it has every time this week, Brandon's voice rings out in my head. 'You remember the accident.' Brandon's limp body falling down to the middle of the halfpipe flashes in my head.

I shake the trepidation off, my eyes on Mia at the bottom. In seconds, she'll be in my arms.

I slide down, straightening my board to drop in, mixing it up so that any competitors hovering around won't know the combos I'll be doing come competition. I twist, my hand reaching to grab my board and the feeling that something's off hits me too late. Too late to land properly and I fly forward, and slide down to the middle of the halfpipe.

My music is blaring in my ears, and I roll over, staring up at the blue sky. *Fuck.*

"Grady!" Mia falls to her knees at my side a minute later, her hands moving over my body, her eyes scrutinizing every inch.

"I'm fine." I unstrap my board and take the walk of shame to the end.

Mia plucks the earbuds out of my ears. "I told you, you're training too hard."

"That's not it."

"You're going to get hurt."

The crack in her voice has me turning to give her all my attention. "Hey." I take off my glove, my hand cradling her cheek. "Don't worry about me. I'm good."

I tamp down the asshole within whose pride has me

wanting to lash out, so I can ease her mind. She's been through too much for me to worry her.

Her hand lands on mine and I catch a few other people coming by, including a medic.

"Are you sure you're okay?" she asks.

"Promise."

"Grady," a medic comes by. "Second fall in two days, come get checked out."

"Second?" Mia asks, her eyes widening. "You didn't say anything about another fall."

"Because it's nothing." I follow the medic over to the station, Mia's boots crunching in the snow behind us.

I'm not sure what she expects from me. She's a snowboarder, she knows the risks.

We head to the first aid station, sitting down as they shine a flashlight into my eyes. Ask me to look up, down, sideways. Mia stands quietly behind them, her arms crossed, unsaid words heavy on her tongue. I will change nothing about my training, this is me and if I want to be the best, I have to be out there as much as possible. Only near perfection wins gold.

"You're good, but be careful out there." The medic slaps me on the back.

Mia and I walk out of the building together, but it suddenly feels like we're miles apart. To make matters worse, Matt Peterson drops in right as we pass the end of the pipe.

"Let's go get coffee," Mia suggests.

"No, I want to see him."

Matt isn't doing anything different than I do down the pipe, but he's got style that I lack lately. I pressure Mia so much to find her love of the sport because it will shine through in her performance, but somehow, I've lost my own.

Matt reaches the bottom and like every time I've seen him lately, he tries the new trick he's named after himself. It's a wobbly landing, but his board hits midway down and he manages to stick the landing.

"Fuck," I mumble.

"He's got nothing on you." Mia tries to make me feel better. "Come on, let's get some coffee."

"I thought you preferred tea?"

She smiles.

"Come on, you need to rest a little."

My eyes stay focused on Matt and a few of his friends congratulating him at the bottom of the pipe. Our eyes meet and neither one of us looks away. There's no challenge present in either of our gazes, but we both know we're each other's biggest competition.

"How about we go back to my place?" Mia whispers in my ear, her breath tickling the skin on my neck.

I turn toward her, dipping her and kissing her. When I have her thinking of anything else but my training, I stand her back up.

"Coffee and then back to training." I swing my arm over her shoulders, grabbing our boards under my other arm and walking toward the little hut they have set up.

"Grady," she sighs.

I don't respond and she doesn't say anything more. She should know by now, training always comes first. How else do I make sure I'm not second best?

CHAPTER TWENTY-THREE

Mia walks out of the bathroom of the suite I rented for the night. She's in a short, red dress. Much shorter than I'd prefer, but if there's one thing I know about Mia, I never have to be jealous. If guys are looking at her it's because her beauty can't be hidden and I would never want to dull her shine. As long as she comes home with me every night, then we're fine.

"You're beautiful," I say, putting on my other shoe.

The neckline of her dress is conservative at least with the bare minimum cleavage showing.

"And you're handsome," she says, grabbing her shoes from her suitcase and bending down to put them on.

Standing up, I straighten my slacks and come up behind her, my hands grip her hips and my dick presses against her ass.

"Keep that up and we'll never make it down there," she says with a giggle.

She stands and I wrap my arms around her waist pulling her back to my chest. Sliding her hair to one side of her neck, my face nuzzles into the crook. "Promise me we'll come up early."

"I promise. Otherwise, I'm sure you'd have me in the coatroom."

I smack her ass. "You know me well."

Grabbing my jacket from the hanger in the closet, I shrug it on and store my phone in the pocket.

"Ready?" I ask, holding out my arm in true gentleman fashion.

Taking her purse off the suitcase, she links her arm through mine. "Yep."

We travel down the elevator, each of us in our own head. After all, our families are about to be reunited and unlike the song says, I don't think it's going to feel so good.

The elevator dings open and when the doors part, the lobby comes into view. I escort her to the ballroom where Gasoline is hosting the event to congratulate their Winter Classic athletes.

"Someone needs to take away his Gasoline I think," Mia says, hearing Dax's voice over the DJ's microphone in the hallway.

"Just take the microphone away."

She laughs and we step into the large room.

"Look who's arrived. Grady Kale and Mia Salter." Dax points to us from the platform setup at the side of the room like he's an announcer at a red carpet event.

You know when you're the new kid at school and you walk into the classroom and everyone's eyes shift to you, judging and appraising. That's what's happening here. I get why they'd look at Mia, she's a knockout, but it's clear that people are wondering what exactly is going on with us.

"Grady." My mom beelines it over to us from the bar area, a champagne in her hand.

"Mom." I step away from Mia but grip her hand to keep her near as I give my mom a kiss on the cheek.

I don't hold her attention for very long, her gaze now cast to Mia.

"Mia, you look beautiful," she says, and the two awkwardly hug, not really sure what direction the other one is going.

"Thank you, Mrs. Kale."

My mom tilts her head. "You know to call me Sue."

Mia smiles. "How are you, Sue?"

My mom takes Mia's hands in hers and squeezes. "I'm good and you? I keep hearing your name on the news right along with Grady's. Looks like you both might go home with gold."

"Mom," I sigh. She knows I hate it when they act like it's a given.

She waves me off. "I'm your mom, I love you no matter what, but you're going to win gold." She looks at Mia. "He's so superstitious."

Mia grants her a soft smile. Who would think they used to be close? Mia was the daughter my mother never had. Mia, my mom, and Mia's mom used to go out for shopping trips and spa days. Boy, have things changed and I can't keep the shame that it's because of me, far from my mind... at least not tonight of all nights when the results of my actions are going to be front and center.

"I guess my parents and Brandon aren't here yet." She scours the room with her gaze, but I don't see them either.

"Can I steal Grady away for a second?" my mom asks.

Mia squeezes my hand but releases it. "Of course."

I lean in close, kissing her cheek. "I'll be two minutes."

Mia's eyes glance to my mom. "Take your time. I see Demi."

Mia's only a few steps away when I overhear her run into my dad. "Oh, Mr. Kale, nice to see you."

"Mia? Is that you?" He pulls her into a hug, holding his scotch on the rocks in his hand. "You've grown into a lovely young woman."

I stop and my mom and I watch the interaction between my dad and Mia.

He whispers something in her ear and her cheeks blush as her eyes seek me out. My dad has always been so welcoming to her. Back in the days when Brandon and I refused to play with her, he'd play her dumb princess games, wearing a tiara and jewelry just like she wanted. They even had tea parties. I never gave it much thought, but I guess to him, Mia was the daughter he never had, too.

"He's always been fond of her." My mom links her arm through mine.

"Yeah."

"So, you two are...dating?" she asks, tucking a strand of her short bob behind her ear.

"We are."

"And how are Bob and Jan with it?"

"I'm not really sure. Brandon isn't happy, but he's agreed to let it go until after the competition."

She scoffs. "Why is it an issue? You did nothing wrong, sweetheart. You had no choice but to continue your career."

My mom, always my biggest cheerleader and the one person who seems blind to my faults.

"I shouldn't have stayed away as long as I did. He was my best friend."

She shrugs. "I don't condone everything you do, but you can't control what happened when Brandon got hurt. I thought we were friends, but they turned their backs on us, too, by refusing our help."

The insult in her voice rings out as clear as it did months after the crash. Personally, I think she's just hurt. Jan and her, were practically like sisters.

My dad says goodbye to Mia and she leaves me with one last smile to last me until I can escape this situation and get back to her.

"Son." My dad's large body pulls me into him and he almost lifts me off the ground. "How are you?"

"I'm good."

He leans into me. "I just talked to Mia. She's as beautiful as ever. You two make a good couple."

"You sure the Salters will let this happen?" my mom asks.

"They have no control over it," I say.

"I'm with Grady. If the two love each other…"

"Whoa Dad, slow down. We just started seeing each other."

He rolls his eyes playfully and smirks over to me like 'get real, man.'

My mom's hands go up in the air defensively. "I'm just saying, they will not like Grady dating Mia."

"I'll talk to Bob, we can't let this feud stop something magical from happening."

Between both my parents, I think my dad might be the true romantic.

Just as I'm about to tell them to just let me handle it, Dax's voice rings out on the microphone again.

"SALTY!" he screams and all heads turn to find Brandon and his parents in the doorway. "Ladies and gentlemen, the infamous snowboarder, Brandon Salter."

Brandon smiles, pushing up his black-rimmed glasses. Mia breaks across the room to hug her parents. Both of their eyes scan the room until they land on us—their enemies—the Kales. This might be harder than I suspected.

MIDWAY THROUGH DINNER, Mia and I have done a great job of keeping our parents from having to say anything more than pass the salt. Yes, our wonderful sponsor was thoughtful enough to sit us all together at the same table.

"So, Bob, did you see the new box store going up right at the city line?" my dad asks Mia's dad.

Mia's knee knocks mine, but I'm not sure how she thinks I can actually stop them from conversing.

"I did, I heard some folks are going to protest it."

My dad cuts his chicken. "I wish them luck. It would put a lot of people out of business."

Bob nods, forking his salad. "That's the truth. Did you hear that the Hendersons went out of business?"

"Really?" My mom looks up from her plate. "That's upsetting. It was always the three of us."

Hendersons being the third most popular B & B in Cedarwood. The fact they went out of business isn't great news for either family sitting here, but it was common knowledge that the Hendersons were never great on the paperwork side of running a business.

"Yeah, they're moving down to Florida now," Jan speaks up, her lips in a frown. "I guess they have college friends there."

"Well, I suppose that's a silver lining," my mom chimes in. "Brandon, how are you doing?"

He looks up from his plate. "I'm good. Going to start teaching snowboarding at Klein's starting next season."

Both my parents look up, surprise and happiness etched

in every line of their faces. "That's wonderful," my mom says.

Jan and Bob look at their son with proud smiles. "They reached out to him and although he won't be teaching any tricks, they think he's insight will be helpful." She gives him a look of warning. "He just loves snowboarding."

Mia glances at me and I want to tell him how awesome it is, that I'm proud of him, but I'm afraid to come off condescending or like I'm talking down to him, so I sit back and take a sip of my water.

"That's wonderful, Brando! You're so great with kids." Mia smiles at her brother.

"Salty!" Dax screams from across the room with a group of snowboarders. He waves him over.

"Excuse me." Brandon wipes his mouth and stands up, leaving his napkin on his chair.

Everyone's gaze follows Brandon until he's nestled into the group of guys giving fist bumps out.

"He's really thriving," my mom says and I close my eyes. "I mean after the accident...what we all feared."

Neither Bob or Jan look up.

"He's great," Jan quips, moving her green beans around her plate.

"I know, that's what I meant..." my mom trails off and Mia's knee hits mine again.

I shrug not really knowing what she expects me to do. Put a partition in front of them?

"Listen, Sue, we're able to live in a small town together, we can surely have dinner together. Let's just stay away from the topic of the accident," Bob chimes in, and Mia gives me a pleading look.

"Can we please stop this?" I say, and Mia's shoulders deflate. "Can we just move on?"

Jan drops her fork, wiping her tense mouth and placing her napkin on the table. "Move on, so you can screw another one of my children over?"

"Jan!" my mom says.

"Sue, I'm sorry, but I can't be on board with this relationship."

"My son is a great person and if he loves Mia..."

"Mom," Mia begs.

Jan looks to her daughter with loving eyes and then to me and all the warmth drains from her expression. "I'm sorry, baby, but what you see in the boy who ruined your brother's career and almost his life, I'll never know."

"Now, Jan, he didn't ruin it." My dad places his fork down.

Jan turns to me, her eyes testing, prodding. What does she know?

Mia swivels in her chair, directly in her mom's line of vision.

"It was an accident, Mom. Grady is really sorry for not coming around and—"

"Forgetting your brother. That's what he did. He went on and got everything that should have been Brandon's."

I watch Bob's hand move under the table to his wife's leg in an attempt to calm her.

"Jan, I can reassure you—" I start.

She places her hand in front of my face. "You have no idea how hard it is to look at you, please do not speak to me."

"I will not allow you to talk to my son that way." My mom throws her napkin on the table.

Mia swipes a tear from her face.

"I'm doing this for your own good." Jan places her hand on her daughter's shoulder. "He won't be there for you long term. He only cares about his own success, that will always come first."

"You're wrong! My son is caring and compassionate. Now, I don't know why he and Brandon lost touch, but I'm sure there are reasons. If Mia can accept them, then I think you should back off." My mom's shaking hand grabs her champagne glass.

"Caring is not a word I'd use to describe your son," Jan says.

"Mom, he was like a second son to you once." Mia is racked with tears and I slide my chair out, but Mia doesn't move.

"Enough," I say a little too loudly, causing people from nearby tables to glance over.

Mia turns around, her makeup smeared down her cheeks. My heart hiccups seeing her this upset.

Jan sits back with a smug look on her face and I see Brandon making his way over from the corner of my eye.

"The accident was my fault. I'm the reason Brandon was hurt."

CHAPTER TWENTY-FOUR

"What?" Mia's small voice says, her watery eyes wide.

"Don't," Brandon's eyes find mine from across the table. "I'm not sure what happened when I left, but this entire feud is stupid. If Mia wants to be with Grady, then leave them be."

"No, Brandon. I'm getting this out." I sit back down and take Mia's hands in mine. "The night of the accident. I'm the reason for Brandon's fall."

"No, you weren't." Brandon fights against what I'm about to say. "Stop it, Grady."

"I can't keep it in anymore." I look from Brandon to Jan. "You're right, I don't deserve your daughter and you shouldn't trust me with another child of yours." Then I concentrate on Mia again. "You know we're competitive, Brandon and I?"

She nods, fear in her eyes.

"I challenged him to do a trick I knew he couldn't land."

"Grady," my mom sighs.

"Fuck that, I would've done the same to you," Brandon says.

"Why?" Mia asks.

"Because, I wanted to be number one." The truth, my truth slips out so easy and simple that it's hard to imagine why it took me this long to admit it to everyone. "I knew it was dangerous for him to try it, but I let him. I didn't back down and tell him not to do it. I pushed him to give it a go, knowing he'd probably end up hurting himself."

The table is quiet, waiting for me to continue. My eyes prick and I blink rapidly. "The reason I never went to see Brandon was because I couldn't even stand to look at him because of all the guilt and shame I had. When they said he would never snowboard again, and I was the cause of it, I just couldn't look at him without hating myself for what I did to him. I was a chicken shit and it seemed easier to stay away."

"But..."

I place my finger on her lips. "Mia, you're beautiful and these last few weeks, you've pulled something out of me...a hope for a life outside of all this. I'll never forget our time together."

Her gaze falls to her lap. "Your mom is right, I'm not the right guy for you."

I stand up, leaning down one last time and kissing her cheek. "Don't doubt yourself up there, you're a talented snowboarder, love the sport and everything else will follow."

Walking away, I head out of the ballroom. Time to pack up my gear and do what I do best. Train. I can't be Mia's number one, but I can be number one on that podium.

AFTER PACKING my bags and hightailing it out of the hotel, I head back to the slopes. The lights are on which means others are there, but at this point, I don't give a shit about lines.

As I get closer, there's only one person still up there.

Matt Peterson.

Waiting for him to finish up, I strap on my board, position my goggles and prepare for my turn. Once he's off the pipe, I press play for the playlist on my phone. It's been the same soundtrack I made up a week ago, but when the first song begins, it's not the one it should be. Having no time to check it, I go with it, thinking I must've pressed shuffle by mistake.

I drop into the pipe, the lyrics of the music taking me far away from my tricks, the beat a tad slower than my usual. By the time I reach the end, I already know that I didn't put this on my phone.

Taking off my gloves, I grab my phone out of my pocket, and when I see what's on the screen, it's like a knife piercing through my heart.

Slow down, Killer, with a heart emoji is listed as the playlist name.

"That was a killer set," a voice says next to me.

Matt stands at the edge and out of all the times we've been thrown together, we've never really had a conversation.

"Thanks," I say.

"Aren't you supposed to be at some sponsor party?" he asks, grabbing his board and starting to walk up the pipe so I follow along with him.

"I need to train if I'm going to be first."

He laughs, his head falling back. "Do you ever have

fun? Actually, scratch that. I think I heard a rumor about you and Mia Salter."

I nod. "Guess the rumor mill is running behind."

"Over already?" His eyes widen. "Story of us athletes, huh?"

He straps himself to the board, and positions his goggles. "Let's see if I can land this trick."

He moves into position, and I sit down with the board strapped to my feet, watching his set.

Damn, he really is good. He gets to the end and again, he can't hold it completely, his hand stretching to catch himself should he fall backward.

Instead of taking a ride myself, I wait for him up on the hill.

"You're not going?" he asks.

I shake my head. "You're coming down wrong."

"No shit," he says, but doesn't seem completely against me helping him.

"As your coming down, stay heavy on that back foot." I stand up. "Watch how I come down this time, it might help you."

He takes my spot on the snow and I insert my earbuds, playing another song that Mia put in my music library.

Just like the previous one, the lyrics keep my mind busy, the beat making it easy to stay in my groove. The last trick I do a 360 with a smooth grip. When I come down, I try to mimic what I want Matt to do.

After gliding to the bottom of the pipe, I wait to watch him. He slides down and drops into the pipe, flawless like every other time. All of his tricks looking like gold material and then he gets to the last one and he lands, not perfect, a tad wobbly, but he didn't fall and his hand never reached down.

"Fuck yeah!" His hands are in the air before he reaches me. "Thanks, man," he says, unclipping from his board. "All this time, and damn, it felt so right as I came down."

I smile a genuine grin, even knowing I gave my biggest competitor an edge over me.

"Do it again, I bet after a few more times, you nail it."

He nods his head, looking over my shoulder. "Why?" he asks.

I shake my head. "I don't want to stand on that platform claiming gold unless I earn it."

"What they say about you is wrong," he points out, a laugh already floating out of his throat.

"Do I want to know what they say?" I ask.

"Probably not, but you're not the selfish prick they say you are."

I laugh, nodding my head in agreement. "Don't tell anyone."

Matt disappears up the hill to come back down.

"No, but you *are* a fucking idiot."

I look behind me to find Brandon, Dax, and Beckett all standing there in their suits and dress shoes.

"What are you thinking?" Dax shakes his head, his jaw cocked to the side. "You just served yourself second place."

I shrug. "Then that's where I deserve to be."

Brandon stays quiet, a smile playing at his lips.

I leave the pipe, rounding the edge to meet up with them.

"I'm proud of you, man." Beckett slaps me on the back.

"I'm not. This isn't how we roll. You don't help your competition," Dax chimes in and my eyes meet Brandon's gaze.

"Yes, they do. We're here to help one another. If you can't beat them then they're better, plain and simple," I say.

"You've lost your mind. First you throw away Mia and now you help Matt Peterson score gold." Dax throws up his arms. "I need a drink."

"Me too," Brandon says, nodding in the direction of the bar.

CHAPTER TWENTY-FIVE

I unclip from the board, holding it under my arm as we head to a bar that's across the street from the village. Once we sit down, I rest my board against the wall behind us because I'm not leaving it outside to be stolen. I rode the best one I have tonight.

"You're being a douche," Brandon says first, his arm already up and ready for the waitress.

I lay my head in my hands. "I'm not winning first if I don't fucking deserve it. I'm done with that shit."

Dax laughs and Beckett slaps me on the back, leaning in closer. "I think he's talking about Mia."

A piece of popcorn hits my forehead and I pick up my head.

"You like her?" Brandon asks me point blank. "I mean, I got the feeling you did on the train, but then things get a little hard and you walk? Again?"

"Bonehead," Dax chimes in.

"Says the asshole who blew his best chance for a good woman at the last Winter Classics," Beckett says.

Dax mocks offense, looking around like I have to be talking about someone else.

Brandon and Beckett exchange a look and Beckett stands. "Let's go, big mouth." He plucks Dax up by the sleeve of his jacket. "This is between them."

Dax's gaze shifts between me, Brandon and Beckett. "I rarely get to razz Grady for being an asshole, come on."

"Next time," Beckett says and then turns to us. "We'll be at the bar."

"Thanks," Brandon says.

I watch their backs until they each sit on stools, Dax still going on about something while Beckett rolls his eyes and orders their drinks.

"I thought you'd be done with running." Brandon leans back, bringing the water to his lips.

I run my hand through my hair. What does he want from me?

"You were right, man, she deserves better than me."

He laughs. "True. I'm her brother. To me, she deserves the perfect male, which you are definitely not. But, there's a problem with that."

"Yeah, what's that?" I twist the cap to my bottle.

"She wants you, or at least she did. I'm not sure now and the longer you leave her with my mom the chances you can get her back grow slimmer."

"She deserved to know the truth."

He nods. "Okay, you told her your version, but you know what I told her? What I told them all? I told them that I was an adult. I made the decision on my own to try that trick *knowing* I might get hurt. It wasn't your fault. Do you think this whole time I didn't know you felt guilty? But, I was feeling sorry for myself and I might've hated you a little because you ended up getting everything I wanted."

"I never meant to fall for her." I sip my water. "I wanted to come visit, but I stole your future. I figured you hated me."

He laughs, shrugging his shoulders. "I'm not going to lie and say it's been an easy road. I was pissed seeing you at the Winter Classics, continuing on without a concern about me. It hurt."

"I'm sorry."

He nods. "I know. I accepted your unspoken apology the moment you hung yourself out to dry tonight. I figured your guilt must be pretty deep inside you to do that."

"What do you mean?" I ask.

"You just destroyed your own life. You self-destructed."

"Your family hates me with good reason."

He waves me off. "I told them that regardless of what they heard, I made that choice and I threw just as many tricks that I didn't think you could land your way that night. We were always too competitive with each other, but I like to think the industry and press did that to us. Always pinning us against one another at the competitions. The running tally of who won what. It was a bomb and that night, it all just blew up."

"Brandon," I sigh. "Still, if I hadn't pushed you so hard or made it impossible for you to back down without losing face—"

"Jesus. Fucking stop." His two hands land on the table. "You can't change it. You can't take back that night. You take back the last four years. You've apologized, I've accepted. Life is way too short for this shit. If you don't promise to forget all of it, then I'm going to walk out those doors and not help you get my sister back."

I smile, remembering how fierce Brandon was when he wanted something done.

"Maybe I need to let her be."

"And make my life a living hell? Fuck you, dude."

I laugh and Brandon waves his hand over to the guys to join us again.

"Hey, man, before they come." I eye the two of them weaving through the crowd. "I am sorry, for everything." I try to convey my sincerity with as much conviction as possible in the hopes that he'll know I truly do hold it as my biggest regret.

"I know."

Beckett and Dax sit down. "So, now you want us back? Jeez, don't I feel small."

"The rumors are correct then?" Brandon asks.

Dax glares up at him.

"Your dick size. Small?"

Dax takes the popcorn bowl and dumps it over Brandon's head. "Fuck off, Salty."

As Brandon gets all the popcorn out of his hair, I think he likes the fact he's back to being with us, as annoying as Dax can be.

"What's the plan?" Dax slams his hand on the table.

"He has to grovel," Beckett says.

"Beg and plead for forgiveness," Brandon adds his two cents and it feels good having him here.

"He has to prove he will not run again?" Dax asks, the question clear in his eyes. "No more of this 'I don't think I'm good enough for you. We're just having fun.' Jerk off or stop fisting your cock, man."

All three of us stare at him like something intelligent just came out of his mouth.

He rolls his eyes. "You know, shit or get off the pot."

"Oh," we all say in unison.

"Clever, Soups." Brandon nods at him.

"Thank you." He swings his arm around Brandon's shoulders. "Salty gets me...you assholes." He shakes his head.

"Back to the problem at hand," Beckett disregards Dax. "You better figure out, and pray to God she hasn't found some accountant to marry."

I narrow my eyes at him. "I don't need any advice from you assholes, I got this one covered."

CHAPTER TWENTY-SIX

The train is loud, everyone talking to someone and the sound echoing around the small space.

Demi gets up from playing bodyguard to Mia. My time has finally arrived.

I get up and slide down next to her. She stands up, but I put my foot on the seat in front of me to hold her in place.

We have about a half hour before we get to Seoul to do a piece with the press where our team will be trying the local food and shopping.

She plops back down, picking up a magazine, pretending to read it.

"I'm an idiot," I start.

"So I've heard." Another flip of the page.

"I'm falling for the most challenging woman ever." She slowly glances over, just her eyes, not turning her head. She flips another page and unless she's some champion speed-reader, she's still very focused on my words.

"Well, I don't think she's too keen on you anyway," she snips.

"I don't think that's true."

"Oh, it is." Her voice holds more conviction than I would have hoped.

"Do you think if I grovel it would make a difference?"

She crinkles the magazine in her hands. "No."

"Beg...pleaded. Because I know we're meant to be."

She closes the magazine and tosses it on the seat next to her.

"No. You left her."

"And I'm really sorry."

She shrugs. "How does she know you won't do it again?"

"She doesn't, but I think I'm a good bet."

She huffs. "She already bet on you."

"I know. Oh, wait." I pretend to get an idea. "Hold on one second."

Demi returns from the bathroom. "Get out, Grady," she says with authority.

"Demi baby, come sit with me." Dax appears, swinging his arm around her shoulders and detouring her toward his seat.

"You're kidding, right?" She glares at him but doesn't circle out of his hold like she could if she really wanted to.

Maybe I was wrong about those two.

Demi peers over the back of the train seat. "If I punish myself by sitting next to this asshole, you better take this one back." She thumbs my way and I smile, holding my hands out in a 'see, even your friends are on my side.'

Mia shakes her head.

"You want it all, right?" I ask.

She turns her head finally and stares blankly back at me.

"The medal, the love, the happily ever after?"

"Doesn't every girl?" she asks.

"I'm not nearly the perfect man you deserve. I'm probably going to piss you off—a lot. You may scream as much out of the bedroom as you do in it. But, I'll make a promise if you take me back."

She waits patiently, her eyes curious.

"They'll be just as many ohhs and ahhs outside the bedroom as inside. I promise to beg for your forgiveness with every move I make. Actually, hold on." I stand up. "Everyone!" I scream before using my fingers and mouth to whistle.

All the commotion stops and eyes focus in on us. She pulls on my coat sleeve to get me to sit back down, but I ignore her.

"I'm about to make a promise and I want you to all hear it."

Mumblings begin and I let my gaze fall to the woman I can't live without.

"I promise to love Mia Salter with my entire heart. I promise to adore her, to seduce her, to pleasure her, to challenge her."

Hoots ring out, mostly from the guys.

"I promise to make sure she's fully satisfied at all times and to admit when I'm being a dickhead."

Mia's cheeks pink.

"What do you think? Should she take me back?"

There's a mixture of yes's and no's, but there's only one answer I really care about.

"What do you say, Mia? Will you snowboard into happily ever after with me?"

She says nothing for a moment and I hold my breath, hoping this works. If it doesn't, I'll think of something else because I won't stop trying. I'm not going anywhere again.

Finally, she seems to come to some decision in her head

and she opens her mouth to speak. "How can a girl refuse that?"

I smile wide, the weight lifting off my shoulders. My lips land on hers as we fall to the bench seat.

She breaks the kiss. "Be gentle with me, Kale."

"Always and forever."

EPILOGUE
MIA

"More," I pant.

Our sweat slicked chests glide along one another, Grady's strength and endurance on full display as he pins me to the wall, pushing in and out of me, my legs hanging over his arms.

"You're the best workout." His classic smirk is on full display and shining right at me.

"Right back 'atcha." I pull his lips to mine, never getting my fill of him.

His tongue dives into my mouth, searching for mine. Instantly they connect and an electrical current runs through my body. There's nothing better than this man and his labored breaths in my ear as he takes me.

My insides clench around him when he drives in deep. "I'm close, faster, baby." My fingers run along the short hair on the back of his neck.

A low growl rumbles up effectively hitting my eardrum, which sends sensations running right between my legs, and I lose the fight, tumbling into my orgasm as all my body's tension vanishes.

"Oh, Grady," I say, but he's not there yet and he pushes inside of me hard before his body twitches and the entire weight of his body presses me against the wall.

"Shit, baby, you're perfect."

Bang.

Bang.

Bang.

"Fuck." We both glance at the clock each of the village rooms have in them.

"Oh, crap." He lowers my body to the ground, rips off the condom, spilling half of its contents on the floor.

"Grady!" I screech.

"Yeah, jackasses, time for you to make your debut," Dax screams through the door.

Neither one of us responds, but from how thin these walls and doors are, I guarantee he heard me screaming.

"Shit!" He grabs my roommate's towel from the back of a chair and wipes it up.

"That's not mine!" I yell, pulling up my panties and pants.

"Well, it's either that or nothing."

I shrug. Point made.

He grabs his boxer briefs and starts dressing.

"I can't believe I let you distract me," I say, shrugging my sweater over my head.

"I think you're the one that jumped me."

True enough, but if Grady Kale was yours, I guarantee you, you'd be living in a constant state of want like I am.

Running over to the mirror I put some more blush on, freshen up my mascara and lip-gloss while he gets into his boots, sitting down and tying them. I take a minute to admire him, still shocked he's mine.

"You can stare at me later, babe, get your boots on," he says without even looking up.

"I wasn't staring."

He glances over to me with that smirk I love so much. I clench my thighs shut. Later.

"I like you staring," he says.

My body loses all muscle control and I almost collapse to the ground. He pulls his hat over his head, and then hip bumps me away from the mirror.

"You're beautiful no matter what, but we gotta get going. I have to make sure my cheering section stays packed."

I tie my boots, throw my arms through my jacket and place my hat on.

Grabbing the strings of his hat, I tug him toward me. "I wouldn't mind if that cheering section had fewer girls in it."

He chuckles his amusement. "Don't be jealous. You know I'm a one-woman man."

I bring my lips to his. "And I'm a one-asshole kinda woman."

He smacks my ass. "Better be."

We each look each other over. He reaches over to the bed and grabs his gloves, stuffing them in his pockets. "Let's go."

He opens the door. Dax is long gone. We sprint through the empty village building and jog all the way to where we're supposed to meet for the opening ceremonies.

By the time we arrive, our entire team is looking at us with skeptical eyes.

"I swear you'll miss your event." Skylar knocks her elbow into my ribcage.

I bend over to try and catch my breath, Grady doing the

same and stretching his calves on the cement wall. Seriously.

"Just working on our cardio," Grady says, and everyone laughs.

"Okay USA, let's go, which one of you are holding the snowboarding flag?" the coordinator asks.

"Me!" Demi jumps up.

"I should do it," Dax approaches and Demi narrows her eyes like he's about to take her baby.

"No, I claimed it first."

"Here we go." Skylar takes a deep breath.

"Guys," Beckett tries to be the rational one. "How about we flip for it?"

"How about ladies first?" Demi sneers.

"This is why they didn't want women in the Classics. You can't be all 'I want this and that and…'" He covers his head as all the women's hands go up and smack him upside the head.

"Idiot," Grady murmurs.

"Fine." He somehow gets out of our grasps, fixing his hat. "Hold the damn flag, but I'm putting that down in the books as you owing me one."

Demi stands there completely unamused.

I share a look with Grady who rolls his eyes. Dax is annoying and definitely loud, but he's our guy and I think he's about to be hit over the head with more than a large crowd of women's hands again.

"I owe you nothing," she says. "If anything…"

The two walk to the head of the group, arguing the entire way.

"Peace at last," I say, and Skylar laughs beside me.

"Hey." Grady comes up alongside me, his hand finding mine.

"What?"

"I love you," he whispers, placing the lightest and sweetest kiss on my lips. "Gold or not, this is the best Winter Classics of my career."

"I love you." I place my mitten-covered hand on his cheek. "But I want the gold, too."

He picks me up and swings me around in his arms. "Mia Salter, you're going to be the death of me."

I nod. "Yep, pretty much."

My feet land back on the ground with the grace of a princess and he bends down and kisses me with the surety and gentleness of a man who loves me. He slows our kiss, his hand never leaving my cheek.

"So, we're in agreement. A couple of gold medals and a few hundred orgasms then we'll live happily ever after?"

I nod. "Sounds perfect."

The End

For once in this duo, Rayne was the one who came up with the idea for Bedroom Games! Of course once she brought up the idea to do a series set and released around the Olympics, Piper hopped on board. Many scenarios went through our heads. Since Piper is from Canada, hockey was originally supposed to be the sport represented. It only makes sense, right? But Piper insisted Team Canada win hockey gold and Rayne wanted Team U.S.A. to win and when we couldn't agree we scrapped that idea. Just kidding! We had it all sketched out, but as things often do with us, our creative brains took over an it all changed...

Rayne was doing research and came across a movie called, The Crash Reel, a documentary on Kevin Pearce, who was an up and coming snowboarder and Olympic hopeful for the 2000 Games. If you haven't watched it, we certainly recommend it! Kevin fell while training on the half-pipe and suffered a traumatic brain injury and was never able to snowboard competitively again.

That sparked the idea for the enemies to lovers trope and then we added in the brother's best friend angle because that's always fun. What happens when two best friends grow up wanting the same thing and only one of them gets it? Born was the story of Grady, Mia and Brandon.

As with all of our books, without the following people, we wouldn't be able to do what we love.

Letitia from RBA Designs for the amazing covers and for putting up with how nitpicky we can be.

Ellie from Love N Books for line editing. I think we might start calling you MacGyver because you always seem to get us out of the bind we put ourselves in, which is no easy task. Thank you!

Shawna from Behind the Writer for her eagle eye proofreading skills and saying its okay when we change the turnaround time with zero notice. (Who knew iBooks now requires your manuscript to be uploaded TWO WEEKS in advance and not ten days. LOL)

Social Butterfly PR for their organization of the cover reveal, tours, parties and everything they're doing for us. You ladies are easy peasy to deal with and don't mind harassing us for what you need. We like that.

All the bloggers who carved out time to promote us and/or read and review the book. Thank you for choosing to spend your time with our words when there are so many awesome options out there.

All our early ARC readers, first for wanting to read our stuff early, their enthusiasm and for posting their reviews.

And of course, all our unicorns. <3 We'd never be here without you. Thank you for loving (or hating) our characters as much as we do. And always letting us try to prove your assumptions wrong (aka Dane, Jagger, and dare we say...Dax!?).

Dax is up next and let's just say he's a love him *and* hate him kind of guy. Trust us, there's a lot of good under that humorous façade! Sometimes men just need to be pointed in the right direction. 😉

xo,
Piper & Rayne

ABOUT THE AUTHOR

Piper Rayne, or Piper and Rayne, whichever you prefer because we're not one author, we're two. Yep, you get two established authors for the price of one. You might be wondering if you know us? Maybe you'll read our books and figure it out. Maybe you won't. Does it really matter?

We aren't trying to stamp ourselves with a top-secret label. We wanted to write without apology. We wanted to not be pigeon holed into a specific outline. We wanted to give readers a story without them assuming how the story will flow. Everyone has their favorite authors, right? And when you pick up their books, you expect something from them. Whether it's an alpha male, heavy angst, a happily ever after, there's something you are absolutely certain the book will contain. Heck, we're readers, too, we get it.

What can we tell you about ourselves? We both have kindle's full of one-clickable books. We're both married to husbands who drive us to drink. We're both chauffeurs to our kids. Most of all, we love hot heroes and quirky heroines that make us laugh, and we hope you do, too.

www.piperrayne.com